He'd Have Liked Nothing More Than To Climb Right Into That Shower With Her, But He Had Things To See To.

A baby to deal with.

Normally he'd have hesitated to enter the room where the baby slept, but anxiety and adrenaline pushed him into the room. He leaned over the crib and looked down at the tiny, red-faced occupant. "Hey, little man, what's the matter?"

Bobby stopped crying. And then he smiled. Not a tentative smile, but a wriggling, fist-waving, feet-kicking, face-splitting grin.

Marty's throat grew tight. A shaft of the familiar pain speared his heart, but he forced himself to reach down and slide his hands beneath the baby, lifting him up and settling him against his chest. The baby snuggled in as if he belonged there.

Maybe he did. Marty blinked, trying to clear vision suddenly suspiciously blurred. This child was a member of his family, *his* child now.

Dear Reader,

Happy New Year from Silhouette Desire, where we offer you six passionate, powerful and provocative romances every month of the year! Here's what you can indulge yourself with this January....

Begin the new year with a seductive MAN OF THE MONTH, *Tall, Dark & Western* by Anne Marie Winston. A rancher seeking a marriage of convenience places a personals ad for a wife, only to fall—hard—for the single mom who responds!

Silhouette Desire proudly presents a sequel to the wildly successful in-line continuity series THE TEXAS CATTLEMAN'S CLUB. This exciting *new* series about alpha men on a mission is called TEXAS CATTLEMAN'S CLUB: LONE STAR JEWELS. Jennifer Greene's launch book, *Millionaire M.D.*, features a wealthy surgeon who helps out his childhood crush when she finds a baby on her doorstep—by marrying her!

Alexandra Sellers continues her exotic miniseries SONS OF THE DESERT with one more irresistible sheikh in *Sheikh's Woman*. THE BARONS OF TEXAS miniseries by Fayrene Preston returns with another feisty Baron heroine in *The Barons of Texas: Kit*. In Kathryn Jensen's *The Earl's Secret,* a British aristocrat romances a U.S. commoner while wrestling with a secret. And Shirley Rogers offers *A Cowboy, a Bride & a Wedding Vow,* in which a cowboy discovers his secret child.

So ring in the new year with lots of cheer and plenty of red-hot romance, by reading all six of these enticing love stories.

Enjoy!

Joan Marlow Golan

Joan Marlow Golan
Senior Editor, Silhouette Desire

Please address questions and book requests to:
Silhouette Reader Service
U.S.: 3010 Walden Ave., P.O. Box 1325, Buffalo, NY 14269
Canadian: P.O. Box 609, Fort Erie, Ont. L2A 5X3

Tall, Dark & Western
ANNE MARIE WINSTON

Published by Silhouette Books

America's Publisher of Contemporary Romance

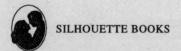 SILHOUETTE BOOKS

ISBN 0-373-76339-5

TALL, DARK & WESTERN

ANNE MARIE WINSTON

has believed in happy endings all her life. Having the opportunity to share them with her readers gives her great joy. Anne Marie enjoys figure skating and working in the gardens of her south-central Pennsylvania home.

For Harold, who keeps all my parts in working order.

Prologue

When he saw the letter addressed in a looping, unfamiliar feminine handwriting, Marty Stryker withdrew the mail from his post office box in Kadoka, South Dakota, as if it might be poisonous. Stopping by the trash barrel in the corner to get rid of the junk mail, he held up the envelope, weighing it in his palm.

Should he even read it? The last few had been so goofy he hadn't even bothered to answer them. Quickly, he slit one envelope and scanned the contents.

Dear Rancher,
How much would I have to know about children
to marry you? I am eighteen years old. I know
you might think that's a little young but—

With a snort, Marty tossed the letter into the trash. *And another one bites the dust.*

Dispiritedly, he pushed open the heavy door and stepped out into the icy winter afternoon. His truck was parked at an angle just a few steps away on Main Street and he quickly strode over and folded his big frame inside, starting the engine and sitting there for a minute while it warmed up. He took off his hat and tossed it onto the seat, running his fingers through his gold-tipped curls.

A mild depression settled over him. He'd placed an ad in several Rapid City, South Dakota, papers nearly a year ago for a wife. Who'd have thought it would be so difficult to find a good woman?

He reached for the keys and cranked the engine, then started the drive south out of town to the Lucky Stryke, the outfit he worked with his brother Deck. All Marty wanted was a capable, friendly woman to share the raising of his daughter and help with the work around the ranch. Someone who'd enjoy a good romp between the sheets a few nights a week. She didn't have to declare undying love; in fact he wouldn't even consider marrying anyone who did.

No, he'd had love once. And losing Lora had been unbearable. All he wanted now was a partner, someone he liked enough to live with and make a life with. He didn't want more children, so she'd have to be someone who didn't hanker after babies. But other than that, he didn't have a lot of requirements.

Or maybe he did. He thought back over the past few months to some of the disastrous encounters he'd had. Drunken women, priggish women, women who said they were thirty when they were closer to sixty...the one that took the cake, though, was the one who had declared that she could never live in a Godforsaken place like Kadoka.

He loved his little town, with its population of seven hundred something. He loved the wide, flat prairie and the gently rolling hills. He loved the lousy winters and the scorching summers, the stupid cattle and the awesome power of the storms that swept down from the north. He glanced out the window at the eroded outcroppings and peaks of the Badlands that stretched away to the west, stark and strangely beautiful to his eye—

And against his will, he remembered another trip on this very road, over two years ago, heading in the opposite direction at a much higher rate of speed as he'd rushed to get his laboring wife to the hospital in Rapid City.

His hands clenched on the steering wheel and the tips of his fingers grew white. He'd lost the battle with time on the trip, lost both Lora and the infant son she'd carried, and lived with the loneliness and grief every day since. Getting married again wasn't at the top of his list of things he really wanted to accomplish in his lifetime, but he had his daughter to think of. His daughter, his beautiful, totally out of control daughter, needed a mother. And he was tired of sleeping alone, trying to get meals and laundry done in between feeding, branding and birthing calves, tired of the dreary look his home had acquired without a woman's presence.

So he guessed he'd keep on with his ad campaign, even though his brother and his friends thought it was a crazy idea.

The right woman had to be out there somewhere.

*   *   *

Juliette Duchenay dropped the envelope through the mail slot in the Rapid City, South Dakota Post Office.

A full minute later, she still stood in front of the box. What in the world had possessed her to answer a perfect stranger's ad for a wife? She must be out of her mind!

She crossed her arms and stared at the box. She was tiny. Maybe if she took off her winter coat, her arm would fit through the slot and she could fish out her envelope. It was illegal, true, but...

She was seriously considering the idea when another after-hours customer walked into the post office lobby. And then another. Clearly her career in crime wasn't meant to be.

Slowly she picked up the infant carrier in which her six-week-old son Bobby slept. Oh, well. Probably the man wouldn't even answer her. Maybe he'd found someone already. The paper she'd picked up had been one of the more ridiculous "meet-a-mate" ones she'd seen in the airport when she'd been coming home from her most recent trip to California. She'd begun to read it for the sake of amusement until it had occurred to her that if she were married, her mother-in-law would have to stop the strong-arm tactics to get her to return to California and move in with her.

Married. It seemed like a drastic step to take, but her mother-in-law was a drastic person. Since Juliette had been widowed, it had been increasingly difficult to make a single decision regarding her own life. She'd gone along with it in the months after Rob's death but now she wasn't pregnant, grieving and exhausted all the time. Unfortunately, when she'd tried to reclaim her life, Millicent Duchenay had gone behind her back and sublet the apartment she'd found. She'd cut off the trust fund that had been Rob's, all the while explaining that it really was best for Bobby if they remained in one home, an extended family together....

And that had been when Juliette had had enough. Moving to Rapid City had seemed drastic at the time. But now she wasn't sure it was drastic enough. Millicent had buckets of money, and money talked. At least, it had talked to the owners of the department store where Juliette had found a job. Her manager had given her two weeks notice along with a quiet warning not to tell her mother-in-law where she was working the next time. She'd gotten another job and heeded his advice. But she was becoming increasingly concerned about her mother-in-law's need for control.

Bobby was *not* going to grow up stifled by his family the way his father had. Oh, she'd loved Rob. But they'd met while they were at college and they'd married suddenly before moving back to the town where he'd grown up...where his mother still lived. Would she have married Rob if she'd seen how tightly he still was tied to his mother's apron strings? She'd never wanted to think too much about the answer to *that*. She'd loved Rob. Of course she'd have married him anyway.

Maybe.

Millicent was a high-maintenance mother-in-law. They'd never had an open disagreement, largely because Juliette had used every ounce of tact and restraint she'd owned when dealing with the older woman. When Rob had died, she'd gradually come to see that Millicent would rule her life if she let her.

So she hadn't.

Moving more briskly now, she headed for her car, attaching Bobby's seat to the base that made it a safety restraint in the middle of the back seat. As she slid into the driver's seat, the ad that had started all the trouble caught her eye:

"Single white male, thirties. Prosperous rancher seeks hardworking woman for marriage, household management, child care. Offers security, fidelity and comfortable lifestyle."

The message had stuck out among the others because it was so straightforward. This man didn't advertise himself as Mr. Romantic, ready to shower a woman with love and affection. He didn't specify a bra size for his applicants, or an age. He didn't care whether they liked a moonlit stroll or red roses, ballroom dancing or candlelit dinners. And most important, he must have children if he needed child care. So he probably wouldn't mind one more.

But she hadn't mentioned Bobby in her letter. Some newly cautious instinct had told her to wait.

Marty Stryker tore open the envelope and read the single, hand-written note he'd found in his post office box in Kadoka, South Dakota:

November 29

Dear Sir,
I am writing in response to your advertisement for a wife. If the position is still available, I would like to be considered. I am twenty-four

*years old, have been married and am now a
widow. I believe I could cook, clean and run
your household. I am interested in children and
would be happy to care for yours. If you would
like to meet, I presently am living and working
in Rapid City.*

   I look forward to hearing from you.

Sincerely,
Juliette Duchenay

December 5

Dear Mrs. Duchenay,
*Thank you for your letter. I have a four-year-old
daughter and I need someone to help care for
her. I also need help with my house since I am a
rancher and am out working a lot. I would be
happy to meet you in Rapid. A Saturday or Sunday afternoon would be best.*

Sincerely,
Todd Martin Stryker, Jr.

December 12

Dear Mr. Stryker,
*It was a pleasure to hear from you. I look for-
ward to hearing more about your daughter and
your ranch. Could we meet in the food court at
Rushmore Mall on Saturday, Dec. 27 at 2:00
p.m.? I am blond and will be wearing a black
dress.*

Sincerely,
Juliette Duchenay

December 20

Dear Mrs. Duchenay,
*Please call me Marty. Sat. the 27 at 2:00 p.m. is
a good time for me. I look forward to meeting
you then. I will be wearing a brown Stetson to
help you identify me.*

Sincerely,
Marty Stryker

One

The woman caught his attention the minute she walked into the café food court at the Rushmore Mall in Rapid City, South Dakota. Not because she was particularly well endowed, which was usually one of Marty Stryker's preferences in feminine company, but because she was so beautiful.

Beautiful, he thought again. Not just pretty, definitely not cute, but breathtakingly gorgeous.

She was tiny, probably not more than five feet tall, and so dainty she looked as though a good wind would send her sailing. As she stood in the middle of the walkway near the food court, a weak ray of winter sunshine fell through one of the skylights, illuminating her pale blond beauty and for a moment, all he could think of was that she looked exactly like an angel.

She was fine-boned, with just about the biggest blue eyes he thought he'd ever seen, and her shining hair was smoothly caught in some kind of fancy twist at the back of her head. She had a straight little nose and a lipsticked pair of bowed lips that reminded him of a perfect china doll. The simple black dress she wore emphasized her fair coloring and a slender, almost childish figure beneath the fabric. She glanced at him once, a flash of intense blue, then looked away, and a hint of rose slid along her high, slanted cheekbones.

Marty was charmed. And turned on. He hadn't had a woman in…how the heck long had it been, anyway? It was a real bad sign when a man couldn't even remember the last time he'd had sex.

But he hardly had time, not to mention the lack of opportunity. Single women weren't exactly thick on the ground around Kadoka, and the few who were interested in accommodating a man weren't the kind he wanted to get anywhere near. After all, he was a father. He had standards.

But man, oh, man, wouldn't it be great if she were the one— *Whoa, horse.* Marty caught the thought before he could complete it. He didn't need a beautiful wife. In fact, he'd already met beautiful women, much more his type than this little angel, in his quest for a wife. None of them had worked out. He'd promised himself he wasn't going to be so picky next time. There weren't that many women answering his ad for a wife that he could keep on looking for the perfect candidate.

And he wanted a wife. Not just for the sex, but for the company. God, he missed sharing simple things like picking out birthday gifts for Cheyenne, drinking morning coffee and conversation.

Then the angel turned his way again. Her eyes locked on his and her eyebrows lifted in a tentative question. She started toward him and he remembered that his wife candidate had said she'd be wearing black.

His heart rate picked up a beat. He stood, whipping off the Stetson he'd worn to identify himself to the woman he was supposed to meet.

"Mr. Stryker?" She was standing in front of him now.

He nodded, not sure if his vocal cords would co-operate if he tried to speak.

"I'm Juliette Duchenay." The angel held out her hand. Then she smiled.

Marty hoped his face didn't show the shock to his system as he slowly reached out and enfolded her fragile fingers in his much larger, anything but fragile palm. The smile transformed her from classically lovely to drop-dead beautiful, bringing a mischievous sparkle to her eyes and displaying white, perfect teeth. Her smile had a pixieish quality to it, a genuine friendliness that he found he liked. A lot.

"It's good to meet you." It was the first thing he could manage to say, the first words his tongue would wrap themselves around as his palm swallowed hers. She had the tiniest hands he'd ever seen, and the skin was as warm and soft and feminine as he'd imagined.

There was an awkward silence.

Marty roused himself from his bemused stupor. He usually was smooth as silk with the ladies and proud of it. Mrs. Juliette Duchenay would think he was a tongue-tied prairie clod if he didn't start talking.

"Would you like to sit down?" There. That was a start.

"Thank you." The faintest touch of pink rose in her cheeks again. A discreet tug made him realize he still was holding her hand and he let her fingers slide away from his, an unsettling feeling of regret lingering. He'd liked holding her hand. The color in her cheeks deepened as he held a chair for her, and he wondered if the skin there felt as baby-soft and fine as it looked. She smiled at him as he seated her at one of the small white tables. "Thank you for wearing your hat. It made you easy to find."

He nodded, not about to tell her that he'd done this nearly a dozen times with prior candidates, all of whom had been unsuitable. "You're welcome." He indicated the food counters ranged around the walls beyond the potted palms and white pillars. "Would you like something to eat or drink?"

"No, thank you." She shook her head. She glanced at the elegant gold watch on her slim wrist. "I'm on my break, so I don't have much time. Why don't we just talk?"

He nodded. Took a deep breath. "Why did you answer my ad?" *Why would a woman like you need to marry a stranger?*

Delicately arched eyebrows drew together in a perplexed expression. "I…it was an impulse, if you want to know the truth."

"And how are you feeling about the impulse now? I'm not interested in something short-term, Mrs. Duchenay. This would be a permanent arrangement."

"Please call me Juliette. I'm still interested, Mr.—Marty."

Her eyes were soft and luminous. He could look into those eyes for the rest of his life without any trouble, any trouble at all.

"Good." He wanted to take her hand, to touch her again. God, her skin was soft. Was she that soft all over? He could hardly wait to find out.

"So," he said. "You work in the mall."

"Yes," she said. "And you're a rancher."

Even if he hadn't put his occupation in the ad, he knew it wasn't a hard call. His skin was tanned from his work outdoors, especially since they'd had a mild fall until the recent big snow. No, as he surveyed his big mitts, he saw there was no way anyone could mistake his hands—scarred from encounters with cranky cattle, barbwire, buffaloberries, splintered wood and hammers that missed their mark—for a city boy's.

"Beef or sheep?" his pretty lady asked.

"Beef. My brother and I have an outfit near the Badlands. Our ranch is called the Lucky Stryke."

"Have you always lived there?"

"All my life. Are you from this area?" He was pretty sure she wasn't, but he couldn't figure out where her accent might have been from.

She hesitated for a moment so brief that he could have imagined it. Then she said, "No. I've only been in Rapid City a short while. I was born in California but my family moved around a lot so I don't really call anyplace 'home.'"

"Where do you work?"

"At the moment, in a women's clothing shop. But

I'd really love to work in a bookstore. Of course, I'd never make any money because I'd spend it all on books.''

Marty laughed. ''I know the feeling. What do you like to read?''

She shrugged. ''Just about anything I can get my hands on. All types of fiction, nonfiction, magazines...my only requirement is that it be well written and gripping.''

''So that leaves out cereal boxes,'' he said.

She smiled again, and again it hit him like a physical contact from a fist. Had he ever seen a woman as classically beautiful? As vibrant?

''Don't bet on that,'' she said, and it took him a moment to remember they were talking about cereal boxes.

There was another small silence, and he smiled at her across the table, enchanted with her feminine presence.

She shook her head. ''I can't believe you have to advertise for a wife.''

He shrugged. ''There aren't that many women who want to live in the back of beyond with a lot of cows.''

''Exactly what are you looking for?'' she asked him. ''What do you want a wife to do?''

Marty hesitated. Then he shrugged. ''No point in sugar-coating it,'' he said. ''I work long hours, mostly outdoors. I need someone to keep my house clean and in good shape, wash and mend clothes, make meals and take care of my daughter. Maybe plant a garden in the summer and help with the stock sometimes.''

Her eyes widened. ''I'm willing to work and I like

to cook but you might have to teach me a few things about gardening and animals.''

So she was a city girl, just as he'd suspected. ''I could do that.''

''How old is your daughter?''

''She'll be five next June. Her mother passed away two years ago and—'' The expected pang of grief and guilt clutched at his heart as it always did, and he suppressed the flood of emotion that threatened. ''—and she really needs a woman's hand,'' he finished quietly.

Juliette nodded, her face serious and sympathetic.

Marty shrugged his shoulders, wishing he were another man in another time, meeting this woman without all the baggage that came with his life. Then he immediately was overwhelmed by guilt. How could he even be thinking stuff like that when he'd once promised to love Lora forever? Until death. He wanted to squeeze his skull between his palms until all the contrary notions settled down. ''It doesn't sound very attractive, I know—''

''It does to me,'' she said.

He stared at her. ''It does?''

''I think I'd like being a housewife.'' She smiled. ''That is what you mean, right?''

''Yes. Although I think the politically correct term today is 'domestic engineer.'''

She laughed. ''I like the sound of that.'' Then she glanced at her watch again. ''I'd better be getting back to work.''

''Afraid you'll get fired?''

She smiled serenely. ''No. I'm a good saleswoman.''

"Do you like it?"

She shrugged. "It's a job. One of life's necessary evils."

"Unless you marry me." Spoken straight out like that, it sounded so...intimate. His mind shot right to dark nights in a warm bed.

She raised her gaze to his, and for the longest moment he forgot everything around him and just let himself wallow in those eyes. Was she thinking what he was thinking?

"I really have to go," she said softly, rising.

As she started out of the food court, he grabbed his hat and followed, taking her elbow when they reached the central walkway that led back to the rest of the mall. After the crowded café area, it seemed positively spacious.

He could feel the fragile bones of her arm beneath his fingers and the warmth of her skin. She seemed tiny walking beside him, and he acknowledged the attraction knotting his gut, making his body stir in response. His heart still belonged to Lora, but his body knew she'd been gone for two years. No question about it. "I'll walk you back to work," he said.

"All right." She smiled up at him. "It's just down this way."

They strolled down the mall, passing specialty shops that sold jewelry from the Black Hills, apparel for women in the family way, sunglasses and leather goods.

Her feet slowed as another store on the far corner of the square into which they walked came in sight, and she paused just outside the entrance. "This is it."

He looked from her to the displays in the windows,

and into the quietly elegant shop behind her. "*This* is where you work?"

"This is it," she said primly.

He felt a slow flush begin at his neck as the stirring in his jeans became a potential embarrassment. The sign proclaimed, "Hidden Pleasures," and he could see why they wanted to keep it hidden. Juliette worked in a store that sold women's underwear! And not just any women's underwear. Filmy, see-through stuff, edged with ruffles and lace, cut into amazingly brief garments, trimmed in satin and velvet—underwear that made a man dream of a woman wearing it. Or not wearing it.

"Marty?" Juliette was smiling that smile that wiped out all his brain cells.

He looked down at her, feeling sheepish and embarrassed. "Sorry," he said. "I was just a little surprised."

She put out her hand. "Will I hear from you again?"

Would she hear from him again? Did the earth rotate around the sun? He needed to spend a little more time with her before he was sure, but he already could imagine Juliette in his home.

"How about a drink after you get off work?" he asked. "We could get to know each other a little more."

Her smiled faded and anxiety carved a little crease in her brow. Then it cleared. "Well, maybe just one short one," she said. "I have some things to take care of at home."

"All right," he said. "See you at—what time?"

"Seven. I'll meet you right here." She turned to

enter the store, then peeked at him over her shoulder and raised her fingers to wave before she walked away.

And he was damned glad her back was turned because there was no way he could control the way his body reacted to that little smile. Hastily he swung away and headed down the mall, willing himself to think of anything, everything, except women and bedrooms.

And his upcoming date with Juliette Duchenay, manager of a sexy underwear store and his potential wife.

He reappeared at twenty minutes before seven.

Juliette caught sight of Marty through the windows of the store as she rang up a purchase and bagged items for a customer. He had settled his large frame on one of the benches in an arrangement of fake trees in the center of the wide walk-through, and as she watched, he opened the bag he carried and pulled out a book.

She didn't know what she'd expected from a man who would advertise for a wife, but Marty surely was the last man she'd ever have imagined would need to do such a thing. He was incredibly handsome. Unlike her own straight, nearly cornsilk tresses, his hair was a chestnut-colored halo with wayward curls tipped by shining gold, the color probably enhanced by the hours he spent outside on his ranch. His hat lay on the bench beside him, and there was the suggestion of a hat ring crimped into his hair.

His eyes were the purest sky-blue she'd ever seen, made even bluer by the tan that made his skin glow.

He wore a heavy leather jacket, but beneath the practical jeans and Western-style workshirt his body was broad-shouldered, slim-hipped and long-legged; in short, incredibly sexy.

She'd looked over her shoulder one last time after she'd waved at him earlier and caught his back view moving off down the mall. His jeans molded his butt and encased his muscular legs and she wondered what he'd be like as a lover. *That* thought made her pause.

Was she seriously considering marriage to a perfect stranger?

She already knew the answer. If it had been any other man in that food court, she'd probably have been polite and friendly and told him she'd made a mistake. After all, she'd had misgivings the very day she'd mailed her letter, and when she'd received an answer she'd nearly chickened out altogether.

But now…now everything had changed.

When her gaze had met Marty's for the first time in the food court, something had pulled into an almost painful ball in her abdomen and she'd had to remember to take another breath. Had she ever been attracted to Rob like this? She must have been once. Of course she had been. The twin strains of widowhood and motherhood probably just had dulled the edges of her memories.

Sex appeal. That's all it was. And she should be dismissing it as fast as she would have with any other man. But now she'd met Marty, and found that the man beneath the appealing exterior was every bit as appealing in personality.

She liked him. She liked him a lot.

Of course she did, she thought as she moved to the

back of the store to assist another customer. Why else would she have called her baby-sitter and asked her if she'd mind staying later than usual tonight? She normally was fanatical about getting home to Bobby. And a part of her felt torn even now. Before he'd been born, she couldn't imagine the powerful maternal feelings that dictated her every move. Now...she thought of nearly everything in terms of how it would affect her son.

She must be crazy. But Marty appealed to her in a powerful way that she couldn't resist, couldn't walk away from. He seemed like such a good man. He'd make her son a wonderful father. If she didn't reach out and take this chance, she could be missing something important. Something that could change her life forever.

The last few minutes until closing time stretched interminably until finally the last customer was walking out of the store.

Marty lifted his head, and his gaze sought hers. When her eyes locked with his, she drew in a breath. He didn't smile, didn't move, but that look seared her with an unspoken possessiveness and deep in her stomach, nerves she hadn't known existed began to hum with awareness.

The moment vibrated between them long after the exchange of gazes ended. He waited while she locked the heavy barred doors of the shop, and then he escorted her to the parking lot. He invited her to go with him to a popular watering hole whose name she recognized from overhearing the conversations of some of her co-workers, and when she asked him if she could follow his truck in her own car, he didn't appear to mind.

The bar was large and noisy and crowded. Marty settled her at a small table next to the dance floor and went to the bar. When he returned with the soda she'd requested, she was surprised to see that he carried one for himself.

Apparently he noticed, because he said, "I have a two-hour drive home tonight. No drinks for me."

She nodded. "Good practice."

He indicated the energetic couples doing a two-step around the dance floor. "Do you do this?"

She shook her head. "I've watched, but no, I've never tried it."

"Then it's time you did." Marty clasped her wrist and started for the floor.

"Marty! I'll step on your toes!"

He stopped and looked back over his shoulder, and his lips curved, then parted as he laughed. "You're just a little thing. I'll hold you high so your feet don't touch the floor."

She smiled and let him pull her out amid the dancers, but when he faced her and held out his arms, she suddenly realized she would be stepping into the embrace of a man she barely knew. *Other women do it all the time,* she told herself. *It's just dancing.*

But deep inside she was afraid that with this man, it might be much more than that. And when his arm slipped around her waist and his brawny strength encircled her, it felt so right that she automatically relaxed and let him lead her.

They danced several dances. Marty taught her the steps, patiently reminding her until she had mastered his movements. He was a strong lead; all she had to do was stay loose and let him put her where he wanted her.

She was very conscious of the words of one romantic song, and when Marty pulled her in and tucked her head under his chin, she could have stayed there all night. They swayed to the three-step, waltzing slowly on the crowded floor, and she fought the urge to press herself closer, to burrow into his warmth and strength and let him take care of her.

"There's something I've got to ask you." His voice was a low rumble above her head, and she tilted her face up so that she could see his expression.

"What?" *Yes, you can kiss me. Please kiss me!*

Marty lowered his head until his lips brushed her ear. "Do you wear that stuff you sell?"

His tone was deep and husky, and his hands drew her even closer as his lips lightly caressed the outline of her ear. Arousal rushed through her so fast that she sagged against him; his arms tightened and his hands slipped over her until she was held flush against every inch of his big body. Every *hard, male* inch.

She swallowed. "I guess you'll just have to wait and see." *Good heavens, Juliette! Whatever possessed you?*

His feet stopped moving for an instant. Then he twirled her in a deep turn again, molding her body to his, and she heard him chuckle. "All right. Do you have a time frame in mind here?"

She gazed up at him. "A time frame?"

"For a wedding," he prompted. "I'd like to marry you."

She opened her mouth. Then she shut it again without a word. Heavens! She'd expected to have more time to think about this. "I'd like to marry you, too," she said, "But—"

"How does Friday sound?" he asked her. "I can get the license and make the arrangements, and we'll start the new year with a wedding."

Her eyes widened. "This coming Friday? That's—that's soon!"

He nodded, smiling at her reaction. "I don't have a reason to wait. Do you?"

She started to say yes, but the word wouldn't come out. "Well, uh…I guess not."

"Good." He took a deep breath and, held as she was against him, the action lifted her clear of the floor for an instant before he set her down again. Automatically she glanced at her watch. It couldn't be nearly nine. Could it? Good heavens, she had to get home to Bobby! Ruefully she thought that a week could have passed while she was in Marty's arms and she wouldn't have noticed.

"I have to go," she murmured regretfully.

"Yeah, I'll be sorry if I don't get going, too."

But he made no move to let her loose.

Finally she stepped back, slipping her hands from his. "I really do have to go."

Marty reached over the railing separating the dance floor from the tables and snagged his jacket and her long winter coat, holding it for her to slip on before he shrugged into his own. Then, as if he'd been doing it for years, he took her hand and led her out of the bar to the parking lot, where they'd parked their vehicles not far from each other.

He walked with her until they reached her car, stopping beside the driver's door, still holding her hand in a loose clasp.

"Juliette…" His voice was low and hesitant.

"Yes?" She realized she was whispering.

"I feel like I've known you a lot longer than just one evening."

She nodded, glad that he was feeling some of the magic that she was. "I know."

He stepped closer, took her hands and placed them on the shoulders of his jacket, then pulled her against him. "I'm going to kiss you," he said.

And as his head blotted out the stars, and the warmth of his arms around her banished the chilly December air, she wondered what she'd have done if he hadn't. She wanted to feel his mouth moving on hers worse than she'd wanted anything since she was about five and she'd thought she would die if she didn't get that doll at Disneyland.

His breath feathered across her cheek, and then the kiss she craved began as his lips settled onto hers. The sensation was exquisite. His mouth was warm and firm as it moved over hers, and she slipped her arms up around his neck, offering herself to him in a wordless motion that he clearly recognized.

She'd missed this, the warm physical pleasures two people could share. But as Marty's tongue flicked along the line of her lips, outlining the shape of her mouth, she had to be honest with herself. She didn't ever remember feeling quite so shaky, trembly, totally turned on before.

Then his mouth grew bolder, and she stopped thinking as she parted her lips, letting him in. He gathered her closer so that she could feel the arousal confined by his jeans and her breasts were crushed against his chest. She twisted slightly, whimpering a little into his mouth in an unconscious plea for more, and he answered her, bending her backward over his arm. His mouth devoured hers, burning a hot path down her throat as he nuzzled beneath her open jacket, over her throat. He nipped at her collarbone, and she shivered in his arms. Then his mouth slid lower, grazing the upper swell of her breast. He raised a hand and brushed aside the fabric of the little black dress and he was suddenly, shockingly, suckling her breast right through the lacy fabric of her bra.

She arched against him, gasping at the sharp, exciting sensation. Between her legs, an aching throb demanded satisfaction, and she squirmed against him until she was half-astride his thigh.

And then he lifted his head. He went completely still and so did she. He shifted her so that she was upright, facing him, and they both made small sounds of protest as she slid over the rigid flesh at his loins.

She realized her fingers were gripping his hair so hard it must hurt. His chest was heaving, and every muscle in his big body was like steel. Deliberately she relaxed her fists and slid her hands down to rest against his chest. As sanity returned, embarrassment set in. What was Marty thinking of her?

"We're standing in a parking lot," he said through gritted teeth. He sighed and pressed his forehead to hers. "The things I want to do to you, *with* you, aren't going to happen in a parking lot or any other public place. And they aren't going to happen until we know each other better."

"Thank you," she said quietly, wondering if the

heat in her cheeks was producing a glow in the evening light. His restraint touched her. "I don't—this isn't the kind of thing—" She stumbled over the words, because they weren't true. She *did,* and she *had,* and very possibly she would have, with him.

"I know." He pressed a kiss to her brow. "I know. It's not my style, either." Then he placed a gentle finger beneath her chin and tipped her face up, inspecting her as she stared back at him, wide-eyed. "Do you have a piece of paper and a pen?"

"Um, I think so."

"Write down your phone number for me."

"Oh. All right." He released her so she could dig through her purse, and she quickly did as he requested. "Here," she said, handing him the slip of paper. It was still hard to breathe evenly, and she saw the flash of his grin light up his face.

"Glad I'm not the only one who's having trouble recovering," he teased, and she had to smile back. Then he drew her into his arms again, holding her loosely with his hands linked at her back. "I'll call you this week."

"I won't be home until late each evening," she said. "Better wait until after nine." It wasn't true, but she wanted to be able to savor his call, and it would be hard to keep her attention undivided if Bobby was awake.

"All right. Then we can talk more about Friday."

"Marty…" She couldn't keep the troubled note from her voice. "Friday is awfully soon. This is crazy!"

He nodded. "If we were teenagers with no experience, I'd agree. But we're adults. I've been thinking of remarrying for quite a while, and I know what I want.'' He leaned his forehead against hers. ''I want *you.*''

And I want you, her heart answered. *I love you.* She barely stopped herself from uttering the words and she stood stock-still, too shocked to move. Could she really be in love with a man she'd met a few hours ago?

Of course she couldn't. Infatuation, that's what it was. Nobody fell in love that fast.

Did they?

He unclasped his hands and turned her toward her car. When she pulled out her keys, he took them from her and unlocked the door, then helped her in with a chivalrous grace that would have charmed her if she hadn't fallen so hard already. ''Think about it and let me know.''

He leaned in and took her lips in one final kiss, thrusting his tongue between her lips and demanding her response until she was straining forward as far as her seat belt would allow, trying to get closer to him. But long before she was satisfied, he drew his head away. His rough fingers caressed her cheek, and then he stood back, shutting her door and waiting until her engine started before he strode across the lot to his pickup truck.

She watched him climb in, then realized he was waiting for her to move before leaving the lot, and she was touched by his thoughtfulness.

A squirming little sensation of guilt wormed its way into her euphoria, though, as she took a left out of the exit and drove toward her apartment. She hadn't told him about her baby.

She would, she assured herself, evading the guilt. It was just that everything had been so new, so special. So perfect. She'd been prepared to graciously back out of the meeting, had had no intention of actually considering an arranged marriage, but once she'd met Marty...

Dreamily, she smiled as she parked near her building. She'd tell him about Bobby soon. And she was willing to bet she was worrying for nothing. Marty must be a good father to his daughter, to be going to such lengths to improve her life. Surely he'd be equally good to her son.

Two

On Sunday morning Marty drew straws with his brother to see who got the unenviable task of replacing some rotting H-braces along one fence line in the larger winter pasture. It had warmed up after the five inches of snow they'd had last week and they were going to get as much done as they could before it snowed again.

Even when he came up holding the shorter piece of hay, his good mood couldn't be banished.

Deck eyed him with suspicion as he handed Marty the post-hole digger. "You look like the village idiot. Something you want to tell me?"

"Nope." Marty lifted tools into the back of his pickup as Deck laid a coil of barbwire beside them.

"Only thing I can think of that makes a man smile

like that is a woman. Just what'd you do in Rapid City last night?''

''None of your business.''

Deck chuckled. ''I knew it! You were with a woman.''

He sure had been, but he didn't intend to tell his brother about it yet. It was still too new, too...special to share.

He hummed under his breath the whole way out to the pasture, eyeing the brilliant color of the wide-open sky and seeing no signs of storms.

No question about it—last night had been the best thing that had happened to him in a long time. He knew in his bones that he could convince Juliette to marry him on Friday. He was as excited as a little kid, thinking about the coming weekend.

No, he took that back. He was excited, all right, but no little kid ever felt the way he was feeling every time he thought about her slender frame, her soft lips and wide, blue eyes. All the signs pointed to a high-pressure system that wasn't going to leave anytime soon.

Well, he could wait. Just barely, but he could wait until Friday to make love to Juliette.

His hands stilled on the post he was setting into the hole he'd dug as he allowed himself to consider what he was thinking. This was the first time since Lora's death that he'd thought seriously of a woman. He'd thought about marriage on a purely objective level, and the steady sex that would come with it had been an abstract until now. Oh, he'd had sex a few times—a *very* few times—in the two years since he'd buried his wife, but he'd never planned it and the women hadn't been important, just interested in a good time.

Making love. That was a troublesome phrase.

He'd made love with Lora. Made love *to* her. Well and often, during the nine and a half years of their marriage. She'd been the first and only girl he'd ever had, and he'd loved her. Oh, how he'd loved her. He'd thought he couldn't get any happier when they'd married, a week after graduating from high school, but he'd been wrong. When Cheyenne had been born, his happiness had doubled.

His spirits dimmed as he thought of Lora's pregnancies. He'd wanted a houseful of kids—his and Lora's. But it wasn't to be. She'd had three miscarriages before Cheyenne came along.

And then…then she'd gotten pregnant again. She'd had a little spotting early on, and the doctor had cautioned her against any strenuous activity. They'd both been afraid of losing this baby the way they'd lost the earlier ones, so Marty had made her stay in Rapid with a friend of theirs for a few weeks. But things had gone so well that she'd soon come home again, and as she'd grown bigger, they forgot they'd been concerned.

When the unthinkable happened, it couldn't have been at a worse time. Lora had gone into labor two months early with no warning. He was out rounding up stock at a pasture much farther from the house than he usually worked. She'd come bouncing across the pasture in his old truck to find him, which couldn't have been good, and they'd raced for the hospital.

But they hadn't made it. Her labor had been fast

and frightening. Three-quarters of the way to Rapid City, Marty had to stop on the shoulder of I-90 and deliver the baby himself, a son so small and fragile it seemed a miracle he was even breathing. Lora had bled and bled...and he hadn't been able to do a damn thing except wrap his too-tiny son in his jacket and race for the hospital.

He'd never forget the final moments of that frantic trip, when her increasingly thready voice had finally quit answering his desperate pleas for her to stay with him, to keep talking to him....

He couldn't bear to dwell on the wrenching hours of the days that had followed, days in which he'd rarely left the hospital, so he returned to thoughts of Juliette.

She was so unlike Lora, who'd been tall and sturdy, with generous breasts and wide hips that should have been able to birth a dozen babies easily. No, Juliette was nothing like Lora. She was small all over, slender and fragile and so fine-boned that he was afraid one incautious movement might snap her right in two.

What would sex be like with her? It wouldn't be making love. Couldn't be, unless he loved her, which he couldn't possibly. Could he? It troubled him to realize that with Juliette, he wouldn't simply be having sex.

No, when he had her soft body beneath his, had her responding to the touch of his hand, let himself drown in the pleasures he knew she offered, he wouldn't be thinking of Lora.

The whole train of thought was so disturbing he abandoned it.

He'd thought about calling Juliette last night when

he'd gotten home but he'd been afraid it might make him look too desperate. As he wrestled the post-hole digger into place for another attack on the gummy prairie sod, he knew good and well he wasn't going to wait another night.

He barely waited until the clock said one minute after nine that evening before he dialed the number she'd given him. It rang twice, and then a breathless female voice said, "Hello?"

"Juliette."

"Marty?"

"Yeah. Hi."

"Hi."

If he'd harbored any doubts about her, they vanished the second her soft voice uttered his name. He closed his eyes and said the first thing that came into his head. "I wish I were there with you right now."

There was a beat of silence, and he kicked himself for being too presumptuous. Just because he felt... connected to her didn't mean she felt the same way.

Then she said, "I wish you were, too."

The soft note of genuine regret in her tone pleased him. "I miss you."

"That's crazy. You don't know me well enough to miss me." There was another small silence, and then she confessed, "I miss you, too."

He took a deep breath as his pulse increased; he had to clamp down hard on the urge to tell her he was going to drive into Rapid City right now. If he hadn't had Cheyenne to think of, he just might have done it. "So how does one o'clock Friday sound?"

"One o'clock?" Her voice was a squeak. "You're serious? You really want to go and get married at one o'clock on Friday?"

"Yep. If you'll have me." He knew he was pushing but suddenly he realized he had to hear a commitment from her, had to know she was going to be his.

He wasn't aware that he was unconsciously holding his breath until she said, "I guess there's no reason to wait," in a timid little tone.

"Great." He was pretty damned tickled that this whole thing seemed to be working out so well.

They talked for over an hour, mostly general getting-to-know-you conversation. He shared everything he could think of about Cheyenne with her. He also began to talk to Cheyenne about Juliette the following day, encouraged when she seemed receptive to the idea of a new mother living in their house.

On Monday he told his brother he was getting married on Friday, and while Deck was still reeling from the shock, he got a promise that Cheyenne could stay with Silver, his sister-in-law, during the day. And he called his bride-to-be again Monday night and Tuesday night.

He told her about his family, his newly married brother and sister-in-law and the closest neighbors, also newly married.

"It was funny," he said. "I was the one who wanted to get married, and it seemed like everybody else except me was saying 'I do.'"

"They're all going to think we're crazy," she said.

"I don't care what they think," he said. "As long

as I get to share a bed with you from dusk to dawn every night.''

He had intended to tease her, but his words backfired as a heavy rush of desire filled him. He'd been mildly turned on since he'd heard her voice; now he had a serious case of circuit overload threatening.

There was silence on her end of the line. Oh, hell. Had he offended her? He had a big mouth. ''I'm sorry,'' he said. ''Can you just pretend I never said that?''

She laughed, a sweet, musical sound that tiptoed along his nerve endings and snuggled into his bones like an old friend. ''Not a chance. I'm going to hold you to it. Dusk to dawn, buddy.''

Now it was his turn to laugh, and it was as much relief that he hadn't angered her as it was delight. ''You little tease. Just wait till I get my hands on you.''

''Okay.''

He groaned.

She said, ''Maybe we'd better change the topic,'' and he could hear the shy smile in her voice.

''Not a bad plan,'' he said. He cast around for something to talk about, but drew a blank.

There was a beat of silence.

''Tell me more about your ranch,'' she requested.

''My ranch. All right.'' He forced himself to concentrate on the conversation. ''I already told you my brother and I own it. We work it together. It's a good-size operation, about thirty thousand acres.''

''Do you and your brother live together?''

''Not anymore. He and his wife, Silver, live in a

cabin that my father built my mother when they were first married but they're building their own place.''

"I don't know very much about ranches or cows,'' she said.

"That's okay. I don't know much about women's underwear, either.''

She laughed, and there was a short pause. "Have you lived all your life on your ranch?''

"All my life,'' he said. "I would never have made it through college. I can't stand being shut up indoors.''

There was another silence. "I enjoy learning,'' she said. "I want to go back to school someday.''

"What do you want to study?''

"Literature,'' she said. Then she laughed. "When I said I liked to read, I wasn't kidding.''

"Were you one of those kids who took a book out on the playground at school recess?'' he teased.

"Guilty. My friends used to get so furious with me because they'd ask me a question three times, and if I was reading, I never even heard them.''

"Remind me not to talk to you when you have a book in your hand,'' he said.

She chuckled. The sound was soft and musical and it made his blood pressure rise, along with other, more noticeable parts of him. "What was your day like today?'' she asked. "I'm trying to get a picture of what your life is like.''

"It was pretty normal for this time of year,'' he said. "I spent most of the day in the neighbors' pasture hunting for three bulls that didn't come in last time we fed. We finally found them. Two were more than happy to come along home, but the third one wasn't so cooperative.''

"So what did you do?'' His life was as alien to her as if he came from another planet. She'd lived in or near a city all her life; Rapid City, which barely qualified compared to L.A. or San Diego, was by far the smallest metropolis in which she'd ever lived. And a real-live ranch…it certainly was going to be a new experience!

He was laughing as he answered her. ''Outsmarted him. He wasn't about to do what we wanted, so we just kept deviling him until he was so tired he finally gave up. After that, he decided maybe going home wasn't such a bad idea.''

A noise from the second floor caught his attention, and he stilled. Sounded like Cheyenne was having a nightmare. ''I hate to cut this short but I have to go. I'll call you tomorrow night, all right?''

"All right.'' Her voice was soft and sweet, and he hated breaking the connection.

"See you Friday,'' he promised.

"All right. Goodbye, Marty.''

Her voice still vibrated along his nerve endings as he raced up the stairs and headed into Cheyenne's room. God, he couldn't wait to see her again!

He called her every night during the rest of the week.

It was silly, she told herself, to be getting so dependent on a little thing like the ring of a telephone at a certain time. Still, she caught herself checking her watch every few minutes, anticipation burgeoning within her as the big hand dragged closer and closer to ten.

They talked and talked, until she winced at the thought of the long-distance bill.

"But soon we can do this in person whenever we want," Marty pointed out.

He told her about his daughter, and she realized the little girl was going to be a challenge. She was four years old and apparently far too good at getting her own way. Well, that would be all right. She enjoyed challenges. And she was looking forward to mothering a daughter. Cheyenne clearly needed her.

They talked about other things, as well. Their childhoods, their families. He knew she had been the only child of a career military man, stopping nowhere long enough to gather moss. In contrast, he told her, he had moss all over him. He talked about his parents and she learned his father was dead and his mother lived in Florida now with a second husband. He told her about his twin sister and brother and all the scrapes they'd gotten into as kids. He told her, too, about the accident that had taken his sister's life, and the misunderstandings and hard feelings that had resulted from it and which only recently had been resolved.

But she still didn't tell him about Bobby.

She didn't know why she was hesitating. After all, he already had a child so she knew he must like kids.

But this one isn't his, whispered an insidious little voice inside her.

She dismissed the unworthy thought immediately. Marty was a kind man, a gentle man. A *wonderful*

man. He needed to know he was going to be a step-
father. But still...

Wednesday night was New Year's Eve. She hadn't
made any plans, and Marty hadn't, either. He called
at ten, and they were still on the phone at midnight
when the new year came in.

"Next year this time, we'll be celebrating our one-
year anniversary," he said.

She hoped so. But she *really* had to tell him about
Bobby. But...Inky, her black Pomeranian, lay curled
against her side as she lay on her bed talking to
Marty. She had yet to tell him about the dog, either.
Maybe she should start small and work up to the
child.

"Um, Marty?" She worked the words in between
a long stream of information about weather patterns
on the prairie. "I have something I need to tell you."

"And what would that be?" His voice was indul-
gent.

"I have a dog." She held her breath, waiting for a
reaction, her pulse racing and her heart pounding all
out of proportion to the simple statement.

"You do?" He sounded a little taken aback. "I
didn't know you were allowed to have dogs in apart-
ments."

"This place allows small animals." Her tension began to dissipate.

"Well, I guess it won't be a problem. He can hang
out with the other dogs around here. How old is he?
Maybe I can train him to work stock." His voice was
beginning to warm.

She laughed uncertainly. "I don't think so. He's um, probably a bit too small for that."

Now his voice sounded cautious. "Exactly how small is too small?"

She took a deep breath. "Eight pounds. He's a Pomeranian. Eight pounds is a very sturdy size for a Pom."

"Eight pounds?" His voice was incredulous. "Good grief. The other dogs'll think he's a meal. He'll make the horses nervous and then they're liable to step on him. No—" his voice was decisive "—that's too small. You'll have to find a home for him in town where he can be somebody's pet."

"But...but I can't just give him away!" Her voice began to quaver despite her best efforts to stay calm. Give Inky away? He'd been her best friend all during her pregnancy and the sad days after Rob's death. Marty didn't understand. He'd been so...so *dismissive*. "He was a wedding gift from my husband."

Dead silence was the only response from the other end of the phone.

Gathering her resolve, she began to list Inky's attributes. "Besides, he's not an outside dog, anyway. He stays indoors. He rarely barks and he's even paper trained if I can't take him out. He's big enough to go up and down the steps and jump on and off the furniture without help—"

"You let him get up on the furniture?" If he could sound more shocked, she couldn't imagine it. "We've never let our dogs in the house. They sleep in the barn when it's cold." His voice was adamant. "You can't have a dog in the house."

Suddenly he didn't sound like the warm and easy-going man she'd spent last Saturday night with, the man she'd been talking with just a few minutes ago. Tears welled up and she swallowed, hurt stinging her heart. He hadn't even *listened* to her!

If he were like this about Inky, how would he react when she told him about Bobby? The idea was daunting. Maybe this whole notion of marriage was ridiculous. She wanted to marry him, wanted it badly, but maybe—

"Juliette?" His voice was so hushed she nearly didn't hear him for the thoughts clanging around in her head.

Finally she realized he'd spoken her name aloud. "Yes?" The tears overflowed and made cold tracks down her cheek. She placed a hand on Inky's tiny head, gently massaging behind his ears, and he heaved a happy doggy sigh as he snuggled deeper against her.

"Are you crying?"

"No." She gulped and tried to breathe evenly.

"Yes, you are." His voice registered cautious concern. "Look, I'm sorry. I didn't handle that very well. Can I have another try?"

He sounded endearingly humble, and she could imagine the look in his blue eyes, earnest and penitent. "Of course. I'm sorry, too."

"I guess one little dog in the house isn't such a big deal," he said, and she could almost hear him trying to talk himself into the idea. "Just because I've never kept a dog in the house doesn't mean it's a bad thing. I know lots of people who do."

She had to chuckle despite herself. "Oh, Marty, maybe getting married without knowing each other better isn't such a good idea after all. I mean, what if—"

But he didn't let her finish. "Hey, sweet thing, one little almost-disagreement doesn't mean we should give up. Don't get yourself all worked up about this, okay?"

"I'm not. Not really. But—"

"But you're still marrying me on Friday," he pressed.

When she didn't respond immediately, his voice lowered, going warm and intimate. "Angel, we're going to be good together. In a lot of ways. I can't wait for Friday to get here so I can hold you again."

"I can't wait, either." And she couldn't. She needed Marty's arms around her, his kisses that made her forget about all her worries.

It wasn't until she hung up that she remembered she still needed to tell him about Bobby. But…he'd had an awfully strong reaction to the dog. What if he decided he didn't want to marry her?

Her stomach trembled. She wasn't sure marrying so quickly was wise, but she *was* sure of one thing. She loved Marty Stryker. Against all common sense, she'd given her heart to a man she barely knew, and if he walked away she'd never be able to forget him. If she told him about Bobby, she risked driving him away.

On the other hand, she reminded herself with forced cheer, the odds were at least as good that he'd be thrilled to have a baby boy to raise. Why shouldn't he? She fell into a troubled sleep still undecided about what to tell Marty about her son. And *when* to tell him.

* * *

Despite the nightly phone marathons, the week seemed to last forever. Juliette's hours at work moved like cold molasses, though her schedule remained unchanged. At home she packed her things into boxes to go with her out to the ranch and separated her few things from the furnishings that had come with the apartment. She gave notice and apologized to her boss for the short time frame. She decided that Friday would never arrive, but finally it was Friday morning. She worked her last few hours and then went home to wait. Marty would be arriving in another hour.

Her neighbor had been keeping Bobby while she worked, since she had moved to Rapid City. It had been a perfect arrangement for a working mother and a retiree who loved babies, and she would miss the older woman, who was baby-sitting one final time today while she got married. She had merely told the sitter she would be moving and quitting work, because she couldn't quite figure out how to explain her coming nuptials. The woman might call the funny farm.

It was freezing outside when she went downstairs, though the weatherman had assured his listeners that it was supposed to be forty-one degrees today, positively balmy for early January. She waited in the little lobby of her building for Marty, her long heavy coat covering the winter-white coatdress she'd decided to wear.

He arrived on the dot of twelve-thirty, as he promised when she'd given him directions to her apartment complex, and she watched through the glass insets at the side of the entry door as he came up the sidewalk.

Had he been that big last Saturday? Goodness, he seemed imposing. He was wearing a brown hat with a fringed leather jacket that matched, and his shoulders seemed a mile wide as he mounted the steps.

Butterflies were batting their wings against the walls of her stomach, and she took a deep breath as she opened the door.

"Hello." She couldn't keep a smile from spreading. He smiled in return, and her heart skipped a beat. He was so handsome!

He stopped in front of her. "Hi." His eyes were the color of a summer sky, and as they met hers, all the butterflies doubled their motion. He came forward and took her hands. "I didn't remember how beautiful you are," he said quietly.

She blushed. Oh, she knew she had a pretty face, but to her *beautiful* was a word applied to well-filled-out women whom men turned to watch when they walked down the street. She had no curves to speak of and would only be considered well-filled-out in a group of twelve-year-olds. Come to think of it, she'd seen twelve-year-olds in the mall who wore bigger bras than she did. "Thank you," she said.

He stepped closer, and her heart skipped a beat at the look in his blue, blue eyes. She could barely breathe as he set his hands at her waist. "It's been a damn long week," he said. "Give me a kiss for luck."

His head was already dipping toward hers and his face loomed large. She closed her eyes as his lips brushed over hers, then settled slowly, firmly, on her mouth as he kissed her so sweetly she felt tears come to her eyes.

She loved this man.

He gathered her closer, and she slid her fingers to the back of his neck and toyed with the gold-tipped curls there. He groaned a little into her mouth, drawing back to smile down at her ruefully. "Let's go do this. Then we can think about…other things."

He meant sex, she knew, and her stomach tightened with a delicious tension as she preceded him down the steps and out to his truck.

As he drove her down St. Joseph Street to the courthouse, she thought of Rob, her first husband. They'd been happy together. At least, they'd been happy at first, until his mother had become a third person in their marriage. But she couldn't remember ever feeling this incredibly arousing excitement at merely being close to him. How could she have been happily married for almost two years without ever knowing the feelings that Marty inspired in her?

He put her in the middle seat beside him and drove with one arm around her the whole way. His attitude was courtly and protective, and she felt safe and secure. Finally, after a week of vacillating between a wild desire to see him and a certainty that she was a loony tune, she felt as if this marriage was the smartest thing she'd done in a long time.

As he parked the truck, he glanced over at her and grinned, a devilish grin that lit his blue eyes with a startling sex appeal. "Ready to get married?"

A sudden attack of guilt struck. She'd never told him about Bobby, partly because she couldn't quite figure out how to introduce the topic. There was some small part of her that worried about Marty's reaction. But that was silly. He'd like her son.

Clearing her throat, she said, "Yes, but we should talk a little bit more about ourselves. I—"

"It'll keep, angel." Marty opened his door and slid out, coming around to help her down. As he took her hand, he said, "We'll have plenty of time to talk for the rest of our lives."

He was right. And she probably was worrying for nothing.

The civil ceremony was nothing like the church wedding he and Lora had had, but as he spoke the words that would legally attach him to the petite blonde at his side for the rest of his life, he began to sweat.

He'd chosen this course, had chosen this woman and pursued her. He was remarrying today of his own free will, and there was no reason to feel guilty. But that's exactly how he felt. He'd been thinking of Juliette's charms all week, having erotic daydreams about bedding her and even more erotic nighttime dreams and though part of him knew it was all perfectly normal, another part of him despised himself. He'd made marriage vows before God once already, promises to Lora that should have lasted a lifetime and would have if she hadn't died.

But she had, and he was ashamed of how fast he'd forgotten her.

He was quiet after the ceremony as they drove back to Juliette's apartment to collect her things. *Lora, I promise I won't forget you.* At his side, Juliette was equally quiet, probably suffering from a similar attack of nerves. Her small fingers twisted the platinum wedding band with five diamonds set in it around and around on her finger, and he imagined it felt odd to wear a ring there again. He'd never worn one for fear of losing a finger while roping, a common mishap among cowboys who insisted on wearing rings.

At her apartment, he made an effort to shake off his introspection. "How much do you have to load?"

She shook her head, not quite meeting his eyes. "Very little, actually. The apartment came furnished. I have everything stacked in the hallway outside my door."

So he came up with her, and together they carried down several loads of boxes and suitcases. He realized he'd never even seen the inside of the apartment in which she'd lived, and he had a sudden moment of panic.

What if she was crazy about blue? He hated blue. Not as in jeans, or shirts, but definitely as in paint or wallpaper. It was the one thing he and Lora had never agreed on. She'd have had every room in the damn house done up in blue if he hadn't protested.

He was standing beside the truck empty-handed, thinking idiot thoughts like that one when he heard Juliette behind him again.

"Marty? Here's my dog."

He turned, expecting to see her with a leash in her hand. But instead, she had both hands wrapped around the handle of a relatively small metal crate, as if it weighed ten tons instead of ten pounds.

"This is Inkspot. Inky for short. He's almost three years old." The words fell more and more slowly from her mouth as he looked dubiously at the small crate she was lugging. "He's very well behaved," she said, caressing the top of the tiny head through the bars.

Great. A gift from her first husband. He'd prepared himself to tolerate her little critter in the house, but seeing the thing up close made it a whole lot more real. He reached for the crate with which she was struggling, easily lifting it and striding to the curb to set it down among the other boxes he was packing, and she turned to go back inside while he stacked things in the truck.

That was not a dog. He stared at the little black mop in the crate. It stared back at him with bright button eyes. It was more the size of a large rat than a dog.

It would probably last less than a week on the ranch.

"Inkspot," he muttered. "You've got a stupid name, mutt."

He was almost finished loading the boxes into the back of the truck when she came down for the last time. He turned around to tell her not to lift anything, but when he saw what she was holding in her arms, all the air whooshed out of his lungs. "What the hell is that?"

Juliette stiffened her back, though the astonished displeasure in his tone made her want to turn and run back inside. Her heart sank like a stone to the bottom of her stomach. She lifted back a flap of the blanket to reveal Bobby's tiny features, snugly bundled in a cap against the chill winter wind. "This is my son," she said.

"Your *son!*" Marty's tone was dark, his face incredulous, blue eyes wide and…and furious. She decided to give him a few minutes. She'd known it would be a shock, but he seemed like such an even-tempered, reasonable man that she'd hoped he wouldn't mind too much.

"Yes." She rushed into the speech she'd been working on all week. "He's almost three months old, and he's a good baby. He won't be any trouble. I'll still have plenty of time to do all the chores and be a mother to Cheyenne, as well—"

"You didn't think it was important to ask me if I minded getting a new baby in this deal?" The words cracked like a whip. His face was flushed and angry, and she swallowed the knot of dread that had risen in her throat. He clearly was far more upset than she'd anticipated. After all, he already had one child.

"I…you have a daughter already," she said lamely. "I thought another child wouldn't be a big problem."

His fists were clenched at his sides; he looked as if he wanted to punch something. "You thought wrong," he snarled. Then, all the shocked anger seemed to drain out of him, and she saw agony in his eyes before he turned, bracing both hands on the bed of the truck. "It's not—it's just— Oh, *hell*," he said with quiet ferocity.

She took a hasty step backward. What in the world was he thinking? What had etched that look of indescribable sorrow on his face? "I'm sorry," she said in a small voice. Then the thoughts that had been plaguing her since the drive from the courthouse returned. "It was wrong of me not to tell you about Bobby before the marriage. If you'd rather get an annulment—'' the words nearly choked her but she forced them out ''—I won't argue.''

He turned and glared at her, and for a long, tense moment she thought he was going to agree to an annulment. But then he spoke again. ''We made a bargain and I'm sticking to it.''

Her hands shook as she started her car and followed him out of the parking lot. Relief that he still wanted the marriage warred with worry. What was he thinking about right now? Why was he so furious?

In retrospect she admitted that it had been an incredibly stupid thing for her to have done, keeping Bobby's existence a secret from the man who would be raising him. A headache formed behind her eyes, pounding more and more fiercely with each passing mile.

They pulled off I-90 at Wall for a quick break, and she walked the dog and changed Bobby's diaper while Marty stood by the truck, his back to her. He hadn't even taken a close look at her son, and she started to get a little angry herself. How could he know whether or not he'd like Bobby when he hadn't even seen him?

It was a good thing the drive was a straight shot because he was on autopilot the whole way. Several times during the interminable drive home, Marty's fists clenched on the steering wheel until he had to make a conscious effort to release them.

Memories blew into his brain like tumbleweeds piling themselves up just like the pesky vegetation caught against his fences.

He hadn't discussed children with Juliette specifically because he hadn't been able to bring himself to raise the issue. And since she hadn't, either, he assumed that having more children wasn't high on her list of priorities, either. More children... Hell, he couldn't even bear to be around babies, much less consider having another one.

Against his will he was back in the pediatric unit of the hospital in Rapid.... His wife, his beautiful, vivacious wife, was gone and his infant son was lying in an incubator struggling to live. He barely heard the hushed voices of nursing staff around him or the quiet hum of life-sustaining machines. Grief weighed on him with the force of a heavy snow. *Lora...you should be here.*

But she wasn't. And his life would never be right again. How could he go on without her? He couldn't raise two children alone. *This wasn't the way it was supposed to be, dammit.*

And it hadn't been. His son, his tiny, precious, premature son had simply been too small, the doctor told him regretfully. So there'd been another tiny headstone added to the family plot, right beside Lora's.

He took deep, ragged breaths, refusing to allow the moisture that burned his eyes to turn into a deluge of tears.

What the hell was he going to do? He hadn't even been able to bring himself to look at Juliette's little guy when they'd stopped at Wall. The thought of hearing baby coos and babble made him feel sick.

And then another thought struck him. How was this going to affect Cheyenne?

He'd gone to great lengths to prepare his daughter for a new mother. But he hadn't said anything about a baby. Sharing the limelight wasn't Cheyenne's strong suit.

He recalled the stricken look in Juliette's blue eyes as she'd offered to give him an annulment. It probably would be the best thing for all concerned. But he hadn't been able to bring himself to agree. In the short week since they'd met, he'd come to *need* her presence in his life. Even if she walked away today and he never saw her again, a part of him would always remember, and regret.

Besides, he thought, not only had he gotten Cheyenne all ready for a big change in her life, he'd told half the town of Kadoka he was getting married. He'd even made one of his periodic attempts at picking up the damn house so Juliette wouldn't think he lived like a pig. No way was he getting an annulment.

That little dog was one thing. Annoying, but nothing he wouldn't get used to. But for God's sake—a *baby!* Clearly there was a lot more to Juliette's decision to marry him than he'd known. She hadn't just been overwhelmed by his charm—she'd been checking him out for fatherhood. For her son.

Her son. He shuddered with the effort it took not to scream his anguish aloud. How was he going to stand having some other man's son growing up in front of him day by day?

A son. A stepson, perhaps, but still a son.

Not his. He pounded his fist against the steering wheel in a rare display of helpless rage. Never his.

Three

He was still struggling with grief and anger an hour later when he drove up the bumpy lane to the house. He'd attacked the lane with his usual speed, leaving Juliette to follow at a slower pace. By the time she pulled in front of the house he had most of her boxes unloaded and sitting in the living room.

He watched as she stepped from the car and looked around. Out here, in the quiet space of his ranch, she looked even smaller and more fragile than she normally did. She walked around the back of the car, looking in vain for dry patches of ground that wouldn't ruin her pretty heels, and unloaded the little dog's crate. Then she bent and opened the small metal door.

The little critter came bouncing out, leaping around her legs in paroxysms of delight, occasionally yapping a hoarse little cough of noise. He looked like a wind-up toy, and Marty shook his head in disgust. A rat with fur.

Just then, the two ranch dogs, both Australian shepherds, came around the corner of the barn. Streak, the older one took his time coming across the yard but the younger dog immediately began to bark, a deep, manly "real dog" bark, as he charged across the yard.

Juliette had been reaching into the car when the dog started barking. She leaped out hastily and snatched up the wind-up toy. She backed against the car, and her body language clearly said she was terrified.

Hell. She couldn't be afraid of dogs, could she? She *had* a dog.

The dogs were determined to get acquainted with the mop, which Juliette was holding behind her back. They took the most expedient route to their quarry, which happened to be right over Juliette.

She squeaked once as one dog leaped up, planting his paws on her shoulders, and as Marty caught a glimpse of her face, he was startled by the naked fear in her expression. Abruptly he moved, coming down off the porch and hollering at both dogs to get back.

They obeyed, and Juliette sagged to the seat in the open door of the car. "I'm sorry," she said. "I'm not used to big dogs."

He started to point out that they weren't exactly enormous, but then he realized that to her they probably were. "Put your little dog down. They won't hurt him."

"But—"

Marty saved himself some aggravation by simply

reaching around her for the dog. As he took the black critter from her, it gave a happy yip and started licking his chin. "Quit that, you mutt," he said, "or I'll feed you to the coyotes." He set the little dog down and immediately the two bigger ones surrounded him. But, as he'd predicted, after some initial stiff-legged strutting and butt sniffing, the dogs all relaxed.

Juliette kept a wary eye on the dogs, he noticed. He guessed he couldn't blame her. Her long wool coat had two large muddy spots on the shoulders, and there was a wet streak of dog slobber across one pocket. She unhooked her baby's carrier from the car and hesitated, looking at the dogs. Out of the corner of his eye he could see one tiny booted foot that had worked its way free of the blanket, kicking wildly.

"Come on," he said shortly, unable to speak for the painful constriction in his chest. He didn't offer her a hand, but he stayed beside her until she got to the porch. Her dumb little dog followed her, getting its paws filthy, so short its belly nearly dragged in the mud.

Once she'd climbed the few steps, she stopped and looked around. "This is...spread out," she said.

He read between the lines. "It can get pretty isolated sometimes. The other women around here keep each other from getting too squirrelly." He yanked open the door and motioned her inside.

"Whoa, there," he said, making shooing motions when the dog tried to follow her.

She turned to face him, her features full of dismay. "But Inky's an indoor dog, remember?"

"Not full of mud like that, he isn't." He retrieved the dog crate, setting it in the utility room just inside the door. "He can stay in there until you have time to clean him up," he said with finality, closing the little critter firmly inside.

Her face was still dismayed, but at least she wasn't arguing. She stayed on the rug just inside the door until she'd slipped out of her muddy shoes and coat, silently looking around her.

He knew what she was seeing. The area in which she stood was a part of the large L-shaped kitchen. It led to a smaller room just behind her that held the washer and dryer, the freezers and a sink. There were hooks on the walls with an assortment of grubby hats and clothing on them, and one wall was a door that led to a full bath with a shower for the times he came in filthy.

In the kitchen the remains of the morning meal—cereal—still sat on the table. Damn. He'd forgotten all about that in his rush to get to town this morning. The kitchen was pleasantly decorated in muted-wheat and gold, colors that he'd always liked, but the curtains were pretty dingy, and the rugs and tea towels had seen better days. The counters were crammed with a hodge-podge of stuff that he knew needed to be put away, and the floor was in dire need of a good scrubbing. When he had time.

He turned abruptly, jingling his truck keys in one hand. "I'm going over to Deck's to get Cheyenne. When I get back I'll put the boxes wherever you want them."

She nodded. "Could you show me where I'll be sleeping? I can go ahead and start putting away some of my clothes."

Where she'd be sleeping? He wondered what was

going through her head. All week long he'd been looking forward to this night; where did she think she'd be sleeping?

He picked up the biggest suitcase she'd brought and led her toward the stairs without speaking, waiting until she'd grabbed the infant seat and started lugging it up the steps. He knew it was too heavy for her, knew he should offer to carry it, but he broke out into a cold sweat at the mere thought of getting close to that baby. So he let her struggle up the stairs and then stepped around her, leading her toward the big room at the end of the hall.

"This is our bedroom," he said gruffly. It felt too intimate, standing there in his bedroom with a woman other than his wife. His *first* wife, he amended silently. He pointed toward the wide pine dresser that occupied one wall. "I cleared out some drawers and some closet space for you."

"Thank you." Her voice was subdued.

There was a squeak and rustle from the little carrier as the baby beneath the blue blanket stretched. He could feel panic rising. He hadn't had much occasion to be around tiny babies in the two years since Lora had died, for which he was thankful. Once they started to crawl and walk he was all right, but he could hardly bear the memories that the sight of a tiny baby swaddled in a blue blanket evoked.

He'd even been praying that his sister-in-law's baby, which was due in February, would be a girl. He thought maybe, just maybe, if it were a girl he'd be able to look at it. If it was a boy, it might have to wait a while to meet Uncle Marty.

A memory from those long, horrible days after

Lora's death floated back to him. Lora's sister and mother had been taking turns caring for Cheyenne. Deck had told him to forget about the ranch, and he had. He'd spent every minute of every day at the hospital, just sitting beside his son's incubator in the modest neonatal unit. He tuned out the doctors who spoke of "abnormal pulmonary function," concentrating all his mental energies on the tiny being behind the transparent walls of the incubator.

C'mon, little guy. Don't give up.

But on the third day the look on one nurse's face told him the truth. The woman was performing one of the frequent routine checks on the baby. As she worked, silent tears slipped down her cheeks and fell onto the papers in her hands.

He'd been paralyzed by the sight. And then despondent, as the truth crushed the bubble of irrational hope he'd been preserving.

His son had died that night.

In the hushed hours when everything slept and only the quiet noises of the machines around them kept them company, the tiny heart had slowly stopped beating. A nurse had unhooked all the machines, and Marty had sat in the same rocker where he'd kept vigil, holding his child's body until the sky lit with dawn.

Juliette's baby squeaked again, a thin little cry, and he felt beads of sweat breaking out on his forehead.

God, he had to get out of here!

Juliette looked around the big, plain room she'd be sharing with Marty from now on. She wondered where Bobby was going to sleep but after the way

Marty had reacted, she was reluctant to bring up the baby again. She would wait and look around after he left.

"My brother's wife has organized a get-together for us tonight," Marty told her.

"A get-together?" she repeated cautiously.

"You know. A party."

"Do you mean a wedding reception?" She was horrified. The way things stood between them right now, a wedding reception would be several hours of the worst torture she could imagine.

"A wedding *dance*," he corrected her. "Nothing fancy." His tone was curt. "Just a little get-together in town. I have a baby-sitter coming."

"I don't dance very well, remember? What will I have to do?"

He looked annoyed. "You don't have to dance. You just have to—" he made a frustrated gesture of masculine impatience "—show up. It's just an expression."

So it really was some sort of wedding reception. Juliette swallowed. "But...Bobby's only eleven weeks old. I've never left him with anyone but the woman who kept him while I worked." She stopped. Marty's face was a thundercloud, and it looked as if he was about to throw a lightning bolt her way. "I— suppose that might work," she conceded. She knew she'd been unfair to him, and she was determined not to make more problems. "Does she have any experience with babies?"

"She's got six little brothers and sisters." Marty's face had relaxed a fraction, though she could still feel the tension and anger he'd kept bottled up since this afternoon, and an indefinable something else that she hadn't had time yet to fully figure out. ''She's been handling babies all her life.''

Bobby began to stretch and squirm in the infant seat, and she absently reached in and scooped him up, putting him to her shoulder and rubbing his back as she debated. ''All right. What time do we need to leave?''

''Around eight, I guess.'' And with no more warning than that, he disappeared down the hall.

She started to call after him, a dozen more questions swarming around in her brain, but she stifled the impulse. It was obvious Marty didn't want to be around her. Or her son.

Tears stung her eyes and she hung her head, still rubbing Bobby's back. She heard the truck engine turn over, and then he was driving away. A tear fell onto the white wool of her dress. Only a few hours ago she'd been on cloud nine, dreaming of a new start and a future that held breathtaking possibilities. Now...now she wasn't even sure whether or not she should unpack.

Marty had rejected her offer of an annulment. But could she live like this, with a man who seemed to despise her all of a sudden? True, she'd made a bad mistake, an error in judgment for which she was prepared to make amends. But he didn't seem to want her apologies.

Although he *had* directed to her to a bedroom he clearly intended them to share, so she guessed there was at least one thing he still wanted.

What kind of marriage could they have if they started out with problems like this?

She sighed. *This is your own fault,* she reminded herself.

Putting off the question of unpacking for a while, she decided to take a look through the house. Bobby was cooing now, and she swung him down from her shoulder, holding him up in front of her.

"Well, little man," she said. "Shall we take a look around?"

He seemed happy, as he usually was unless he was hungry or wet, so she decided to wait a little longer to feed him. The bottles and formula were in one of the boxes at the foot of the stairs, anyway.

She started with the upstairs. There was a bathroom off their bedroom and another hall bath that apparently served the other three bedrooms. At the moment, it was full of children's bath toys and toothpaste with television characters on it.

One of the bedrooms was a guest room with what looked like a king-size bed. It was the closest to the master suite so she decided she could set Bobby's portable crib up in there temporarily until she figured out what room to use for a nursery and got it decorated.

The second was clearly Cheyenne's room, decorated with pink and lavender ponies bouncing on the white wallpaper, white-painted furniture, a handmade quilt in similar shades covering the bed, and toys, books and clothes scattered over every square inch of the pink carpet. She shook her head, rather stunned at the mess. Cheyenne had a few things to learn about keeping her room clean, even if she was only four.

The door to the third room was closed and locked. But a short investigation revealed the key on the top of the doorframe. She guessed it was intended to keep Cheyenne out more than any adult.

Unlocking the door and leaving the key in the lock, she stepped into the room.

It was a nursery. She supposed it had been Cheyenne's when she was smaller. No wonder Marty kept this door shut. Seeing the baby things would be a reminder of the wife who'd died and the additional children she assumed they'd planned to have.

The thought gave her pause. That was one thing they hadn't discussed in all the phone marathons of the past week.

Did he want more children? It wasn't something she could ask him now, that was for sure. She'd always planned to have more than one child. And she supposed, in her deepest daydreams of this marriage, she'd imagined they'd have children together, younger brothers and sisters for Cheyenne and Bobby.

But that was hard to picture after the way Marty had reacted to her son. His shocked expression when he'd been confronted with her baby invaded her mind again.

What the hell is that? Hurt rose, and she deliberately focused on the nursery, willing herself to forget it. Things weren't going to be as simple and easy to adjust to as she'd expected. But Marty had said he didn't want an annulment and she didn't either. She wanted *him,* despite the weird way he'd been acting. And she was sure that with time, things would work out.

She looked around the room. It was a bit…fussy for her taste. A jarringly frilly pair of lace curtains hung at the windows, tied back with lengths of blue ribbon. On top of the dresser was an assortment of baby combs and brushes, diapering supplies, tiny socks in white and blue, and basic infant medical supplies. Everything was sorted into little baskets or boxes and neatly arranged.

In the middle of the floor were two boxes with women's coats, boots and sneakers, scarves and gloves in them. A large leather purse was tossed carelessly on one. There was a white crib along one wall, a matching dressing table with a diaper pad on top and a chest of drawers, a diaper bucket full of neatly folded infant blankets, and a white rocking chair in which there sat a teddy bear that was at least three feet tall. Over the corner of the crib was tossed a beautifully crocheted blue afghan.

It looked as if nothing had been touched since the day Lora Stryker died.

She shook her head and looked down at Bobby, cradled in her arm. "I think we won't mention this room for a little while. What do you think?"

His wide blue eyes regarded her solemnly for a moment before his little face crinkled in a toothless infant grin and his whole little body wriggled.

She laughed in delight as his mouth worked and coos burbled out. "Oh, yes? Is that what you think? Okay. Sounds like good advice to me." And then she sighed. If only it was so easy to make Marty happy.

Shutting and relocking the door, she ventured down the stairs. At the bottom was a small entry hall that led to the front door. From the looks of it, that door was never used: there wasn't an ounce of mud on the rug or the porch outside. On the right was a large office she supposed Marty used for business, although

extensive bookshelves filled with a wide range of ti-
tles ran around three walls, and there was a child-size
table in one corner opposite the desk. Atop it was a
big sheet of white paper with crayons spilled across
it.

The living room was across the hall. It was much
like the kitchen, nicely decorated in similar gold-and-
wheat tones with a touch of deep-green, although it,
too, needed a thorough cleaning and Cheyenne had
left her mark with toys all over the floor again. There
was even an upright piano in one corner, to her
delight. She'd studied piano up through her high
school years, and though she would never be great,
she enjoyed playing for pleasure.

Her momentary happiness dimmed as she remembered that all of her music was still in California.
Then she frowned. Too bad. She'd just have to buy
new. She was far from penniless, though she'd rarely
had to use the money her parents had left her. When
they'd married, Rob had told her to invest it for the
children they hoped to have and she had. But now
she was living on the profit instead of rolling it into
the next investment. And she was still grateful that
she hadn't simply handed the money over to Rob to
be taken care of by his family. If she had, Millicent
would have found a way to withhold that like she had
everything else.

Bobby was beginning to make little sounds of distress, so she unearthed his diaper bag and changed
him, then made up some formula and spent a quiet
quarter hour feeding him. Afterward he went to sleep,
so she took him upstairs and put him in his carrier
while she set up the small crib in the guest room. She

moved him into it without waking him, then went back downstairs.

Inky was looking hopefully at her, so she let him out of the crate and took him out for a minute, then cleaned the mud from his coat. She fed him and began sorting out her boxes while he investigated his new surroundings. Fortunately, unpacking wasn't difficult since she'd labeled each box according to which room of the house it should go.

There weren't many, and within twenty more minutes she'd gotten them all into the right rooms. Marty still wasn't back after almost an hour. Just how far away was his brother's house, anyway?

She started unpacking her clothing first, using the drawer space Marty had shown her, putting her things in the bathroom next to his. The butterflies came back. Was this really happening? Had she really married a handsome cowboy she barely knew simply because she thought she might love him?

She *was* insane.

She was in the kitchen, unpacking the most necessary things she'd brought, mostly items for Bobby, when the truck came growling back the lane again. Moments later, little footsteps came pounding up to the back door and her new stepdaughter burst into the room.

There was a palpable aura of energy surrounding the little girl, although she stopped, suddenly shy, just inside the door. Juliette smiled and walked across the kitchen.

"Hello, Cheyenne. I'm Juliette." She knelt and offered her hand to the child. Marty's daughter was incredibly lovely, even at the age of four, with thick black curls hanging in luscious ringlets down her back. Her eyes were wide and blue and she smiled, revealing perfect pearly teeth and twin dimples that were going to drive the boys wild in a few years.

"H'lo," she said. "Are you the one who wants to be my stepmother?"

"She *is* your new stepmother," Marty corrected her gently from the doorway where he'd just entered the house.

Cheyenne's expression changed, and she tossed him a frown over her shoulder. "I don't want her."

He smiled uncomfortably. "Sorry, shortcake, it's a done deal. I bet you and Juliette will—"

"No, Daddy!" She crossed the room and shoved at Marty's knees. "I don't want her!" Then she spun and stomped through the kitchen on into the living room.

A heavy silence fell over the kitchen.

"She's not always that bad," Marty said. "She'll get used to you."

Juliette just stared at him.

A sound from upstairs made her spin suddenly as alarms went off in her head. Bobby! She'd left him sleeping in the guest room, and Cheyenne had just gone up there. At the same instant she and Marty both dashed for the stairs. His longer strides gave him the advantage, and she raced up the steps in time to see the little girl push open the door of the guest room. Marty already was catching up to the child.

As Juliette skidded down the hallway, she heard Marty's voice, stern and angry. "No, Cheyenne!"

Juliette rushed into the room and came to an abrupt halt.

Cheyenne stood beside the portable crib, her small arm grasped firmly in her father's hand. In her small fingers she clutched a large wooden block.

If it had landed on Bobby's tender infant skull... "You *do not* drop things on sleeping babies," Marty said.

Father and daughter glared at each other for a moment. Then her bottom lip came out as her small black brows drew into a straight dark line. "I don't *like* that baby. I don't want him in my house."

Their loud voices startled Bobby; he began to whimper.

Juliette was so frightened and angry she could barely speak, but she knew how important it was to make this child feel as if she still had some control in her own home. "Look, Cheyenne." She attempted to speak quietly and calmly. "He's waking up. If you like, you can help me change his diaper."

Cheyenne studied Juliette for a moment. Then Bobby whimpered again and a crafty gleam entered her eyes. The little girl opened her mouth and let loose a shriek that probably could be heard clear in town.

Bobby's little body jerked and he began to cry.

Marty flinched. Then he grabbed Cheyenne around the waist and swung her under one arm. He strode out of the room and down the hall.

Juliette scooped up Bobby and began to comfort him as she went to the doorway to watch.

Marty went to Cheyenne's door, setting the still-screaming child firmly in her bedroom. "When you're finished and you apologize for screaming, you can come out,'' he told her. Then he closed the bed-room door—not gently.

The door opened almost immediately and Chey-enne, sobbing and screaming, tried to fly into the hall-way, but Marty caught her and shoved her back, clos-ing the door again.

Marty turned and looked at her. ''Let's go down-stairs,'' he said. ''She'll get over it and come out pretty soon.''

Bobby was already drifting back to sleep, sucking on his pacifier for a few moments, then relaxing al-most into sleep before furiously sucking again. She carried him down and put him in the infant seat on the kitchen counter. No way was she leaving him alone up there with Cheyenne.

''Did you get a chance to look around?'' Marty took down two glasses and opened the refrigerator. He withdrew a jug of premixed, presweetened iced tea and poured them each a glass, then offered her one.

''Thank you.'' She nodded. ''I looked around a little as I was putting things away. It'll take me some time to remember where everything is.''

He took a long drink from his glass and she tried not to notice the way his strong brown throat moved as he swallowed. ''Look,'' he said finally as he low-ered the glass and set it on the table, ''I'm sorry about the way I acted about the baby.''

''No, I'm the one who should apologize—''

He raised a hand and stopped her. ''Let me get this out. Please.''

Puzzled, apprehension rising within her at the se-rious note in his voice, she nodded.

"My first wife died giving birth to our son. The baby was premature, and he only lived a few days."

Oh, God. She was so shocked she could only stare at him as his words echoed mercilessly through the silent kitchen.

He stood abruptly and took his glass to the counter, then grabbed his jacket and shrugged into it, keeping his back to her. "I...it's hard for me. Being around your baby, I mean." He turned then and looked at her, and for the first time she understood what the raw agony in his eyes meant.

Oh, dear God. What had she done? She sucked in a breath, feeling her own eyes filling with tears. "Marty...Marty, I am so sorry—"

"I'll be back in time for dinner," he said quietly. And then he opened the door and walked out.

Juliette sat frozen, listening to his booted feet clomp off the porch and down the steps.

Now she realized why the nursery had so much blue in it. They must have known the child was going to be a boy. Without warning, her chest heaved and she pressed a hand against her mouth to keep from giving way to the sobs that wanted to break free.

Was there anything worse in the world than losing a child? She didn't think so. Losing Rob had been devastating. But if something happened to Bobby...the thought didn't bear closer examination.

Why hadn't he told her? She could think of very little that would make this whole situation worse now. No wonder he'd been acting strange. It probably killed him to have to see Bobby, to hear him...she thought of the way he avoided handling the carrier even when it was obvious she'd needed help, the way he'd bolted from the bedroom earlier. She'd thought he was angry. Well, maybe he was, but worse—much worse—he was heartbroken.

And having her son to remind him of what he'd lost was simply fresh salt in a wound that hadn't healed in two long years.

His throat was tight and aching as he saddled his horse. For one long moment he laid his forehead against the smooth leather, his fingers gripping the sides of it so tightly they stung.

He just wasn't sure he could do this.

The sound of Juliette's baby crying had shaken him right down to the tips of his boots. Then the crying had stopped almost immediately when she'd picked the kid up, subsiding to pathetic little snuffling whimpers, and that was almost worse than the crying. His son had never been able to cry. He'd only made those same kinds of weak, helpless sounds.

God, he couldn't bear it. Was this his punishment for failing to save Lora and his son?

He stayed out for the rest of the afternoon, assessing the herd and checking to see which cows looked about to calve. The yearling calves were looking healthy because there'd been so little snow they hadn't had trouble getting to grass, but the weather report for the next couple of days was troubling, and the almanac said February was going to be a killer.

He finally went back to the house around six, after checking the water in the stock tanks. It took every ounce of courage he possessed to walk through the back door, and he didn't begin to relax until his swift, sidelong glance confirmed that the infant seat on the counter was empty.

The smell of something cooking teased his nostrils the minute he entered the kitchen. He recognized it right away—the vegetable soup Silver had given him yesterday. But he also smelled rolls or biscuits baking, and his mouth began to water. How long had it been since he'd come in and smelled someone else's meal preparations? Six months, anyway. Since Deck and Silver had gotten married. At least when his sloppy brother lived here, he'd shared the kitchen duties.

Juliette was at the counter—and to his amazement, Cheyenne was perched on a chair beside her. They were cutting cookie dough with a glass.

"Hey, there," he said, striving for a casual note. "Do I have time for a shower?" He walked over and kissed the top of Cheyenne's head.

Juliette looked up, an expression in her eyes that reminded him of a mare who didn't trust her handler. "Sure. We can eat whenever it suits you."

"Give me about twenty minutes," he said. He hung up his coat and hat and took off his boots, then walked through the kitchen in his stocking feet.

When he returned, in clean clothing, freshly shaved and showered, the table was set and all he had to do was take his seat. The baby was awake again and sitting in the little seat, but it—*he*—was quiet, and Juliette had carefully turned the cradle so that it faced away from him.

It was…a real dinner, like normal families had, he realized. It was a miracle. And she'd even replaced the terrible instant tea with the real thing. But even though things seemed to be working out as he'd planned, at least in this regard, the meal was still far from normal. Juliette was very quiet while they ate, and he let Cheyenne do most of the talking. He knew the two of them needed to set a few things straight, but they couldn't have a conversation with the kid—*the kids*—around, anyway.

He did help clean up afterward, then turned to his wife. "How about if I get Cheyenne ready for bed? We can ease into the changes in her life and you'll have a little time to yourself to get ready for the wedding dance."

She nodded, though her eyes were still wary. "That sounds good." And without another word, she picked up the baby from the carrier and disappeared up the stairs.

He got Cheyenne ready for bed and read her a couple of stories, and by then it was time for him to go get the sitter. He'd heard Juliette on the stairs while he was in Cheyenne's room, and he couldn't find her at first. Then the thin glow of light from beneath the door of Deck's old room caught his eye. Walking down the hall, he hesitated, then knocked lightly on the door, and it swung open at his touch.

Juliette sat propped up on the bed with pillows behind her. She wore a long, dark-blue robe that had fallen open to expose her calves and knees and her small pink toes were bare. She had her baby in her arms and was feeding him a bottle, and she'd been singing something. When the door opened she stopped abruptly. Her eyebrows arched in enquiry but she didn't speak.

For a moment he froze, and he closed his eyes

against the pain. "I'm going to go get the baby-sitter now," he told her.

She nodded. "I'll be ready when you get back. He's almost asleep." She returned her attention to the baby with a tender smile.

The smile stayed with him during the cold drive out to get the baby-sitter and back again. She'd smiled at *him* until this afternoon, and in every smile had been the promise of intimacies to come. But then he'd found out about the way she'd lied to him—or at least, deceived him on purpose—and things had changed between them. Would she let him have her tonight?

His pulse pounded in anticipation. He sure hoped she was prepared to make this a real marriage. She'd known how it would be when she'd agreed to marry him.

At the house he found Juliette ready, as she'd promised.

She told the baby-sitter a little about her son Bobby, assured her that he probably wouldn't wake up again—and all the while Marty stared at her. She was wearing a rose-colored dress with a matching jacket and another pair of those pretty little heels that made her ankles look so good.

He was going to have to get her some boots or she'd freeze those gorgeous gams off this winter, although it would be a hardship to cover up legs like that. But he didn't tell her so.

She finished giving instructions to the sitter and shrugged into another winter coat, shorter than the one the dog had muddied earlier, before he could help her with it. "I'm ready," she said.

Four

When they pulled into the big parking lot, she assumed he was going to get gas at first. But he kept driving around to the side and parked close to a door. When he came around and helped her out, she realized this...this *bar* was the place where this party, this wedding dance, was being held.

As she watched, a couple of cowboys sauntered in, followed by two couples. Every single one of the men wore a hat and *everyone* had on blue jeans. Her heart sank.

"Why didn't you tell me everyone would be wearing jeans?" she asked.

Marty looked blank. "I didn't think about it." He surveyed her dress dispassionately, then took her elbow and urged her forward. "You look fine."

She wanted to cry. She looked more than fine and

she knew it. But she felt as out of place as a swan in a lake full of ducklings as she picked her way across the parking lot. At least it wasn't knee-deep in mud like the yard of her new home.

He yanked open the door and they stepped inside, and every face in the room turned their way. She could feel her cheeks turning hot.

The place was all chrome and black with huge speakers and a microphone at the front of the room. The bar to the right was crowded with cowboys, but Marty led her to a couple standing not far from the entrance. He took her coat and tossed it over a nearby chair, then turned and indicated the pair.

"This is my brother Deck and this is his wife, Silver. This is Juliette."

Deck was a slightly taller version of Marty and his eyes were a darker, deeper blue beneath the brim of his black hat. He wasn't quite as blatantly in-your-face handsome as his brother, but his rugged, formidable good looks were compelling all the same. His features looked as if they didn't smile easily as he took her hand. "So you're really married to my brother. Guess I'd better say congratulations."

"Thank you." She smiled at him and the coolness in his eyes warmed slightly, a glint of humor surfacing.

"I wish I'd met you before the wedding. I could have warned you about Marty—"

"Shut up," Marty growled. There was no amusement in his tone and the grin faded from Deck's face as he stared at his brother with narrowed eyes.

Silver, Deck's wife, stepped into the uneasy silence. "It's so nice to meet you, Juliette." Silver took her hand. She was a lot taller than Juliette would be even in her highest heels, and she was lovely, with a heavy cloud of black hair and the most striking eyes Juliette had ever seen. It was obvious where her name had come from. "That's a lovely dress."

"Thank you." Juliette looked down at herself ruefully. "I'm afraid it's a bit too dressy for tonight."

Silver laughed. "You'll find it's a bit too dressy for *any* night around here. South Dakotans live in Wranglers." She smiled. "I'm originally from Virginia and I still haven't gotten used to the fact that most of my pretty clothes are going to turn to dust before I have a chance to wear them again."

Wranglers. A new dismay struck her. She didn't even own real jeans, just one pair of lightweight denim pants that she'd brought from California. She hadn't been here long enough to need them, since she had dressed up for work at the mall, and the only other clothes she had were unsuitable, being made for California's mild climate.

"Wranglers," she said slowly. "That could be a problem."

"We'll get together in a day or so and have a real visit, and I'll help you get a head start on your cowgirl wardrobe." Silver said. "I probably won't be here long tonight—I'm a bit more tired than usual these days."

Silver was pregnant. Very pregnant, if the rounded shape beneath the black sweater was an indication.

"When are you due?" Juliette asked. It was the first, and most crucial, piece of information most women wanted to know—

"Juliette has a baby," Marty said.

The conversation stopped again.

"Say that again." Deck was clearly used to issuing orders.

Her cheeks were burning, but she forced herself to keep her chin up and smile. "I have an eleven-week-old son. My husband died unexpectedly ten months ago."

Deck and Silver stared at Marty, then turned back to look at her. Their faces were equally dumbfounded, and she was sure she knew why. They probably couldn't believe Marty had married a woman with an infant son.

Silver recovered first. "I'm sorry about your husband," she said. "What's your son's name?"

"Robert, but I call him Bobby."

"I like Robert," Silver said. "We've been arguing over names for months now."

Deck touched his wife's arm. "I'm going to buy my brother a drink. Would either of you ladies like anything?"

Juliette declined as did Silver, and a moment later Deck had hustled Marty up to the bar. Silver suggested that they sit down, which Juliette did gratefully. She felt ridiculously out of place here, in this bare little bar with its metal tables and vinyl-covered chairs and bright neon signs advertising beer behind the bar. She'd never been much of a bar person at all. She didn't drink alcohol except for the obligatory sip of champagne at weddings, and as she'd told Marty the day they'd met, she wasn't the world's greatest dancer.

Someone had taped up big white paper wedding bells on one wall, and a sheet cake covered in white icing was set on a nearby table. It apparently wasn't intended for a grand cake-cutting ceremony, since a cowboy came over and cut himself a whopping chunk as she watched. Frankly, she was relieved. A wedding reception with its attendant rituals could only make this whole mess worse.

And then someone started clanking a spoon against a glass. Within seconds, the bar resounded with the sound of metal clanking against beer bottles as people used utensils, pocketknives and anything else they could find to clang out the signal.

Juliette knew what it meant and her heart sank even lower. It wouldn't stop until the groom kissed the bride. At the bar Marty appeared oblivious until his brother poked him in the ribs and said something, pointing in her direction. Marty shifted his body toward her and their eyes met. Then, unsmiling, he stood and strode her way.

She put out a hand to stop him as he approached. "I don't think—" But it was like trying to stop a freight train.

He grabbed the hand she extended and dragged her to her feet. Then, before she knew what he intended, he scooped an arm beneath her knees and lifted her high against his chest, his mouth coming down on her startled one even as she gasped in surprise.

Her arms went around his neck more out of reflex than passion, but as he kissed her hungrily, she clutched at his shoulders and her mouth opened under his, allowing his tongue to seek out hers in the automatic response she'd been unable to hide since the first time she'd seen him. Her fingers tightened on him and her hands stole up around his neck. How could she love him so much?

And then the bar erupted in cheers and catcalls and whistles. Marty lifted his head with a grin, the first hint she'd seen of his normal good humor since he'd learned about Bobby. "Those suckers will be lining up asking me to help them write ads for wives after tonight. You're about the best-looking thing most of them have ever seen."

The words were a splash of cold water on the moment of passion. "Great," she said, trying to mask the hurt his casual comment had caused. "I'll add that to the list of reasons you married me."

The grin faded from his face. Slowly he set her down. "I told you exactly what I wanted when we met," he said and his eyes were angry. "You're the one who didn't play fair."

She collapsed into her chair as he stalked back to the bar, resting her elbows on the table and putting her face in her hands.

"Juliette?" Silver's voice sounded worried. "You do know about Marty placing an—"

She nodded, dropping her hands and attempting a smile. "I know. I answered his ad. We came to a very civilized agreement about marrying." She looked at Silver and was moved almost to tears by the sympathy in the other woman's eyes.

"He didn't know," she said before she could catch it back. "Marty didn't know about my baby until after we got married today."

Silver's mouth rounded and her lovely eyes widened in evident dismay. "That explains it."

"What?"

"Why he seems so...odd tonight." Silver shook her head. She appeared to be holding a debate with herself for a long moment. Finally she said, "Has he told you about his wife and son?"

"I knew he was a widower," she said quietly. "But I only learned about his little boy after..."

The dark-haired woman put a soothing hand over hers. "You couldn't have known," she said. "I never knew her but Deck told me Lora went into premature labor with their second baby. She had to drive a truck out through the fields to find Marty. He rushed her to the hospital but he had to stop to deliver the baby on the way and she started to hemorrhage badly. She bled to death before he could get there."

Juliette felt as if someone had hit her squarely in the chest. Suddenly, with full clarity, she could understand why the horror of his loss would make it difficult for Marty to talk about it. "And the baby died."

Silver cleared her throat. "Three days later. He was just too little and his lungs weren't developed enough. Marty took it really, really hard, Deck says, but you'd never know it to talk to him. He's covered up his true feelings with wit and charm for years. I suspect that probably started when his sister Genie died. Nobody gets close to the real man beneath that killer smile."

Juliette took a couple of deep breaths, hoping the sick feeling in her stomach would subside. Was there any way she could ever make up for forcing Bobby on him?

The rest of the evening didn't get any better. Marty came over to check on her once in a while but she didn't know what to say to him, so after a few stiff encounters, he hung out by the bar with a gang of men who guzzled beer while she sat at the little table with Silver. She tried not watch him, but she couldn't help but be aware of his unusually quiet presence nearby. She was relieved to note that he wasn't drinking much at all.

Silver's sister-in-law Lyn McCall joined them, and other people came by occasionally to introduce themselves. The speakers and the mike up front, she discovered, were for karaoke, which Lyn and most of the people in the bar pronounced "croaky," a fact that brought the first genuine smile of the evening to her face.

Lyn had recently announced her own impending motherhood, and if Juliette hadn't been so aware of her husband's brooding presence at the bar, she would have enjoyed the talk of pregnancies and babies with the other two women.

"Juliette needs clothes," Silver shouted at Lyn above the caterwauling of one off-key karaoke performer. She glanced at Juliette. "Boots, too?"

Juliette nodded. "Almost everything but underwear."

"We can get jeans in Phillip," Lyn said. "And boots and a coat there, too. Did Marty keep any of his first wife's things?"

"Wouldn't matter," Silver said. "I've seen pictures of her. She was as tall as I am and—" she made an indelicate motion that conveyed exceptional size in the chest area "—well-endowed." Then she gave an enormous yawn. "Sorry," she said, chuckling. "It's getting past my bedtime."

As if he'd heard the words, Deck detached himself

from the group of men at the bar and came over to the table. "Are you ready to go?"

Silver nodded. "And I'm sure Juliette's exhausted, too." She gave Deck a meaningful look.

"Why don't I tell Marty she's ready to go?" He turned on his heel and headed back to the bar.

"We need to get going, too." Lyn stood and walked across the room to her husband, Cal. She stretched on tiptoe to whisper something into his ear when she reached him. Juliette's heart ached at the way the man's arm went around her and his finger tilted her chin up for a lingering kiss.

Then Marty was coming toward her, and they all walked out to the parking lot together.

The air was brisk and biting and a lot chillier than it had seemed on the way in.

Deck pointed at the moon, and Juliette glanced up at the red halo surrounding it. "Snow before morning," he said.

"Oh, great." Lyn shook her head. "Your first week of marriage and already South Dakota's giving you a taste of its miserable winters. Call me if it gets to you."

On the way home, Marty explained that Lyn and Silver were both newly married, also. Juliette was relieved to learn this would be Silver's first winter in the area. At least she wouldn't be alone in her newness.

Cal and Lyn turned off the highway ahead of them, and when Marty turned off a few minutes later, Juliette was pleasantly surprised to realize how close— relatively speaking—Lyn lived. When they arrived at the house, Marty paid the baby-sitter and took her home while Juliette hurried upstairs to check on Bobby.

And Cheyenne, she reminded herself. She was a mother of two now.

She checked on both children. Bobby was still sleeping in the same position she'd left him, lying on his side. He had a funny habit of stretching one leg clear out, and sure enough, his little leg was extended as if he were planning on taking a walk upon awakening.

Cheyenne was sleeping on her back with both little hands outflung. The child looked totally angelic, and Juliette smiled ruefully as she brushed a kiss over the soft cheek. Life wouldn't get dull with this one around. Cheyenne had come out of her room with a whispered apology as pleasant as you please after Marty had disciplined her earlier, and Juliette had taken special pains to include her in the dinner preparations. All in all, she thought their first day together hadn't gone too badly after the initial shock.

She shut the little girl's bedroom door and went back downstairs to let Inky out one last time before going to bed, then shut him in the kitchen. Though he normally slept on her bed, she had a feeling Marty would have a few choice things to say about that. Weary, she slipped off her shoes and carried them as she trudged back up the stairs.

If only she felt as optimistic about her marriage as she did about stepmotherhood. She couldn't imagine how they were going to manage to get through the days ahead if Marty couldn't even bear to be around babies. Tears stung her eyes and she blinked them back. She wasn't a quitter, she reminded herself.

She'd married Marty and she'd keep the promises she'd made in the judge's chamber.

He just needed time to get used to the changes her presence and Bobby's would bring to his life. He had good friends and family who were obviously deeply in love with their wives. Maybe there was a chance that he could grow to love her, too.

Oh, boy. Might as well wish on a shooting star, girl.

Quickly she got ready for bed, but when it actually came time to slide into the big oak bed where Marty slept, she hesitated. She stroked an absent hand over the quilt as she acknowledged the hopes she'd had for tonight, the fulfillment of the attraction she'd felt since the moment she'd seen him. She wanted Marty to make love to her in a way she couldn't ever remember wanting a man in her whole life.

But Marty wasn't here. And worse, when he did come home, he was going to be as quietly miserable as he'd been since she'd come down the stairs from her apartment with her son in her arms.

She didn't want her first night in her new marriage to be like that.

Slowly she turned. Leaving one small lamp burning on the bedside table, she made her way back to the room where Bobby slept and crawled into the king-size bed there.

Marty entered the house after dropping off the baby-sitter to find the place totally dark. In the kitchen, his new wife's little dog gave a halfhearted yip that stopped the moment he said, "Can it, critter."

Then he took the stairs to the second floor. Anticipation had created a steadily growing arousal that burned in his system, and he headed directly for his bedroom—

Only to find his bed as cold and empty as it had been every night for more than two years. Disappointment rushed through him, killing his desire. It was swiftly followed by anger, the only other emotion he could allow himself to feel at the end of this hellish day.

He'd hoped she would be waiting for him. Hoped that perhaps they could salvage something from the collapse of the relationship he thought they'd been building. But apparently Juliette wasn't interested in a relationship with him, except as it pertained to having his ring on her finger. Why in hell had she married him?

She'd hooked him, but good. And he'd fallen for every flirtatious bat of her eyelashes, every swish of those slim skirts across her trim little bottom, every hesitant response she'd given him.

Now it was painfully clear that he'd been the biggest kind of idiot. He'd been so hot to get married before she got away, and she'd had no intention of getting away. She'd been as desperate as he had for this marriage. The only question now was: why?

To gain a father for her fatherless son? He didn't think so. If that were the case, she wouldn't have hidden the kid from him, she'd have checked him out right away to see if he was a good parent candidate....

He felt as if he was missing something important, as if some crucial piece of information was eluding him. *Why* hadn't she been up front with him about her baby?

The answer was suddenly crystal clear, even if the reason behind it wasn't. She *had been* desperate to get married. So desperate that she wouldn't take a chance on jeopardizing the opportunity by scaring away the potential spouse with a baby that wasn't his. She needed to get married.

Now all he had to do was figure out why.

She was in the guest bedroom that had been his brother Deck's, sleeping alone in the big bed with her baby in the little portable thing nearby. He pulled the door almost shut, weariness and sadness tugging at him, and quietly returned to his own room, where he stripped and crawled into the bed he'd hoped to share with his bride.

And his dreams were a restless, anguished jumble of hospitals, red flashing ambulance lights and crying babies.

The house was chillier than usual when Marty awoke in the morning. He dressed and went downstairs to the kitchen and turned up the heat. Juliette's dumb little dog danced around his feet, and he figured if he didn't want it to have an accident he'd better let it out.

It was snowing when he opened the door of the utility room, little tiny flakes that had already piled several inches of fluffy stuff on the ground, and it was cold. Really cold. The thermometer on the porch post read ten degrees, and there was a vicious north wind blowing, which probably meant it was at least fifty below. Damn. He and the men couldn't ride more than a quarter mile in that without freezing solid.

The little dog, Inky, didn't like the cold much. He scampered out, did his duty and ran right back to Marty's feet again.

Marty couldn't help but laugh. ''Good job,'' he told the dog. ''Gotta keep it quick so we don't freeze out here.'' He took Inky in with him, and the kitchen was still empty.

He'd hoped Juliette would be up, but he ate his breakfast and she still didn't appear, so he shrugged into his warm clothes. She probably was wiped out after yesterday. She might need to catch up on her sleep.

He headed for the garage where he'd had the good sense to put the truck last night, and disengaged the heater from the engine block, then went out on a scouting trip.

He drove the ranch roads slowly, keeping an eye out for early cows that might be calving. He and Deck had been trying to get all the breeding cows into pastures closer to the house since the weather was supposed to turn, but some of them were wily old sneaks that managed to elude the men. They would calve out in the snow somewhere and the calves would freeze to death. On the radio, the weatherman was talking about a blizzard developing. One look through his windshield confirmed it. Small flakes like this usually meant they were going to get lots of snow.

Deck was at the barn when he got back and they went down to the pastures to feed.

''Morning.'' His brother's greeting was normal, but the speculative look he aimed at Marty wasn't.

"Morning." He ignored the look. "This looks like it could get ugly."

"Probably will." Deck heaved bales of alfalfa off the back of the truck. "So how's your bride settling in?"

"Fine."

Deck raised his eyebrows. "You all right?"

"Fine." The note of concern in his brother's voice nearly undid him, and Marty set his jaw. Deck had been intimately acquainted with grief since their sister had been killed; he, more than anyone, knew the hell in which a part of Marty had lived since Lora and the baby died. Marty swallowed. "Let it be for now."

Deck nodded his head. "Okay."

They finished feeding and then spent the rest of the morning chopping ice on the dam before heading to their respective homes.

By the time he'd put the heater on the truck's engine at the house, his fingers were numb and clumsy with cold. He stomped the snow off his jeans and boots on the porch but when he reached for the doorknob, it wouldn't open. It took him a full minute of fumbling with the knob before he realized it was locked. And by that time he could see Juliette hurrying toward the door.

She pulled it wide and stepped back so he could enter.

"We never lock doors around here," he barked at her.

"I was here alone with two small children," she said, tilting her little chin in the air. "I'm not accustomed to leaving my doors unlocked."

Damn. He hadn't intended to start off the day on

this note. He knew he owed her an apology, and instead here he was yelling at her. "I was just surprised," he said, peeling off his gloves. His fingers were white with cold and his legs felt numb, too. He hadn't been dressed for this kind of weather when he'd early that morning. "Sorry I shouted."

She was staring at his hands. "That doesn't look good. Is that how frostbite starts?"

His clothes were soaked now that the snow was melting and he shivered. "It'll be all right. I'm going to take a hot shower." He started forward, then stopped again, watching her face as he spoke. "We have to talk."

"I know." But her gaze slid away from his. "Would you like me to get you a hot lunch while you're showering?"

He nodded, grateful that she was making an effort. "That would be nice."

He was halfway up the stairs before he noticed her little dog bouncing along behind him. He started to holler that the damn dog couldn't stay in the house, but then he realized he couldn't, in good conscience, put the critter in the barn where the other dogs holed up when it got this cold. He was just too little; he'd freeze. And if it made Juliette feel more like this was her home, he supposed he could get used to having one small dog in the house. "Just stay out of my way," he growled at the mutt.

When he came out of the shower, the dog was lying on the bed, right in the middle of the clean shirt he'd tossed there before he went into the bathroom. He swore it had a smile on its face and he scowled, yanking his shirt out from under it and sending it rolling end over end across the bed. "Scram, mutt."

The critter leaped off the bed and its nails clicked on the wood floor as it raced around the foot of the bed, but it didn't scram. Instead, it came to stand in front of him, tail waving in a perky arch over its back.

It tagged along at his heels as he walked back down the stairs and into the kitchen. Juliette had a mountain of grilled cheese sandwiches waiting for him. She'd made tomato soup from a can as well, and she poured him a mug of hot coffee. The baby was in its little cradle on the counter again and for a second he marveled at how content the little guy seemed to be most of the time. Cheyenne had been a fussy baby; he could remember taking turns with Lora walking the screaming infant for hours at night.

"How's Cheyenne been?" he asked abruptly.

The question brought the first smile to her face that he'd seen since yesterday morning. "Great," she said. "We built log houses and played with dolls this morning." She went to the door of the living room and called Cheyenne, then took a seat across from him as his daughter bounced into the room.

"Hi, Daddy!" She ran to him and threw her arms around him exuberantly. "Me 'n' Juliette played *all* morning."

"Sounds like fun." He kissed her and set her in her seat.

"An' *I* fed that baby!"

Her little face was beaming, and he knew she expected some comment, so he said, "Good," even though the very word *baby* made him flinch.

Involuntarily he glanced at the infant seat, still facing away from him. Thank God the kid was quiet. It made it easier to pretend he didn't exist.

"What's this?" Cheyenne was sniffing suspiciously at the tomato soup. "I don't like it."

"Tomato soup," said Juliette. "I made sandwiches, too. Do you like cheese?"

Cheyenne nodded. "But I'm not eating that soup."

His daughter crammed two sandwiches down her throat in the time it took him to eat his first one, then demanded to get down and go play. Not feeling like arguing, he merely nodded, and she disappeared.

"You may be excused," Juliette called after her.

"Sorry," he said sheepishly. "I guess her table manners need some work."

"Eventually." Juliette looked across the table at him. "What did you do with her during the day... before?"

"Anything I could," he told her. "Lora's mother and her sister Eliza each took her one day a week. Silver's been doing that, too, since she and Deck got married. I hired a sitter sometimes; one of the hands' wives kept her other times. The rest of the time, she had to come along with me."

"Will she miss that?"

"Not a chance. She hated being dragged around. Although she still can visit her grandmother and her aunt once in a while. I'm sure you'll need a break occasionally."

Juliette gestured toward the window. "It's really cold out today."

"The weatherman says it's supposed to stay cold for a while." He shook his head. "I'll have to go back out this afternoon."

"But isn't that dangerous?"

He couldn't prevent the smile that curled at the corners of his mouth. "If I stopped doing everything on this ranch that was dangerous, I'd be sitting around the house all day."

"What do you have to do?"

"When the snow gets too deep for the cattle to get to the grass, we feed bales as well as cake."

"Cake?" She looked totally bewildered.

"Not birthday cake." He grinned. "It's a supplemental feed."

Her eyes still looked worried, but she didn't pursue the subject.

He indicated the boxes still sitting unpacked on the counter. "Are you planning to finish settling in today?"

"I suppose." Uncertainty colored her tone. "Maybe you should make me a list of things to be done that you think are most pressing."

He stared at her. "Why? The whole house needs help." He shook his head. "You can start wherever you like and do whatever you want. I'm not particular." Then he remembered. "Except that I'm not real fond of blue."

She looked down at the cornflower-blue wool sweater she was wearing with a pair of tan slacks. "You're not?"

He laughed. "I don't mean like that. I mean as in redecorating. Color schemes."

"Oh." She considered. "Not a problem. I can live without blue rooms."

"Good." His relief was heartfelt. Then he looked at her again. The blue sweater made her eyes a deep, intense color that was striking with her fair skin, and her cheeks were a pretty pink. She'd pinned her hair up again; it suddenly struck him that he'd never seen her with it down.

That thought invariably led to others and he shifted in his chair as his jeans became uncomfortably tight. "You look very pretty today," he said.

"Thank you." Her voice was quiet; she studied her coffee mug.

He reached across the corner of the table and took her hand. "I'm sorry we got off to such a bad start yesterday."

Her cheeks colored and he knew she was thinking about *why* they'd gotten off to that bad start.

"Let's talk tonight." He could tell from the look in her eyes that she knew he wanted to do more than just talk, and he kept his gaze steady as he waited for her answer.

Her whole body went still and for a long moment there wasn't a sound in the kitchen. "All right." It was a whisper.

Her nearness was having a powerful effect on his body. He stood, pushing back his chair without letting go of her hand, and pulled her to her feet. She placed both of her hands flat against his chest but he circled her slender body with his arms and pressed her close enough that she couldn't miss feeling what she did to him.

He made a sound deep in his throat and bent his head, searching for her lips. Her mouth was passive beneath his at first and he forced himself to gentle the hungry edge that urged him to devour every sweet inch of her. Her mouth quickly softened in the generous response he was beginning to expect, and he used his tongue to deepen the kiss. Her little hands gradually slid up his chest and around his neck, stroking the skin there and making him shudder with need.

He tore his mouth from hers. "I want you," he growled.

She bent her head and let her forehead rest against his broad chest, and he could feel her breathing as heavily as he was.

He held her a moment more, then lifted her chin and kissed her once, hard, before letting her go. "I'll be back in a few hours," he said.

He struggled into the layers of clothing that would protect him from the worst of the bitter cold again, although his body was so warm he figured he could walk to the barn buck naked and not even notice the chill.

Juliette decided to tackle the kitchen first, since it looked as if that was where she'd be spending a good part of every day. She thought she'd made too many sandwiches, but to her everlasting shock, Marty had eaten every single thing she'd placed on the table. She'd watched him tuck away the food, bemused, wondering whether he'd have eaten more if she'd set it in front of him.

Her body still tingled where he'd held her against him. Was she stupid to be planning on sleeping with him after the misunderstanding that still lay between them? Although Marty had said that this was a permanent decision on his part, before they ever married, she couldn't help but wonder if he still felt that way.

He hadn't so much as looked at Bobby, even when

Cheyenne had talked about him. How could she make a family with a man who couldn't stand to be around her son? Even though she understood his reasons and the pain that must haunt him, it still hurt when he rejected her child. It felt like a rejection of *her,* which she supposed it was, in a way.

The wind still howled around the corners of the snug ranch house but now the tiny ping of ice crystals bouncing off the windows joined the sound. Well, she wasn't going anywhere today, that was for sure. So she might as well get something done in this house.

She went into the living room to see if Cheyenne wanted to "help," a trick she'd quickly discovered kept the little girl too interested and occupied to be objectionable, but the child was sprawled across the sofa, sound asleep. Smiling, Juliette covered her with an afghan and let her sleep.

She started with basics, scrubbing the walls and the floor and tossing the rugs into the washing machine. She put Bobby down for a nap, then emptied the refrigerator after putting the mountain of newspapers scattered on the counter into bags for Marty to take wherever they went to recycle around here. She washed the counters and then started emptying out the kitchen drawers, one by one, and reorganizing after she'd thoroughly scrubbed them as well.

Cheyenne came into the kitchen almost two hours later, yawning, her hair a messy tangle of curls sticking out every which way.

"Hello, sleepyhead," said Juliette.

Cheyenne ignored her, climbing into a kitchen chair and laying her head on the table.

Juliette went to the table and knelt down beside the

child. She wanted badly to cuddle the little girl, but she almost could see tiny porcupine prickles raised and ready. "Cheyenne?"

The child flopped her head over on her arms so that she was looking at Juliette.

"I thought you and I could plan something special to do each afternoon while Bobby is napping. What would you like to do today?"

Cheyenne thought about it for a minute, then slowly sat up, and in a queenly manner that had Juliette hiding her smile, the little girl raised her arms for a hug. When Juliette put her arms around the fragile body, Cheyenne clung surprisingly tightly for a long moment before they each drew back, and Juliette felt tears prickling at the backs of her eyes. She was suddenly fiercely determined to make a difference in this child's life, to give her a normal childhood and all the love she had within her.

"I wanna make cookies," Cheyenne said.

Five

The rest of the afternoon went surprisingly smoothly. They made no-bake cookies with peanut butter and oatmeal. Cheyenne helped for a while and then played with Inky, who quickly grew tired of being wrapped in a blanket and hid beneath the couch. Then she got out modeling clay and played at the kitchen table while Juliette continued to clean the kitchen. Bobby awoke and needed a bottle, and Juliette allowed Cheyenne to feed him for a while. He seemed fascinated by his new big sister, his large blue eyes following her every movement, and he wriggled and squealed when she talked to him.

Juliette threw the rugs in the dryer and took down the curtains, washing them, the tablecloth and all the dish towels she could find in a second load. By five she had everything but the big walk-in pantry reorganized and she was reasonably sure she could find things now. It already felt more like "her" kitchen.

She wasn't sure what time Marty would want dinner, so she'd defrosted a roast and stuck it in the oven with carrots and potatoes. She mixed up biscuits but held off baking them until he came in, since they'd only take a few minutes.

By six-thirty, Cheyenne was getting defiant and cranky. Juliette decided they might as well eat, and she would feed Marty whenever he showed up. What was he thinking, to make a young child wait so long for dinner? The answer was easy. He probably wasn't thinking about it at all. He'd essentially hired her to take care of his child and his house so he could devote more time to the ranch. Still, she thought, he was going to have to get in the habit of letting her know when he'd be coming in.

Cheyenne's temperament improved so markedly after the meal that Juliette was astonished, and she made a mental note to give the child a snack the next day. Bobby was much happier when he ate and slept frequently and regularly, so it stood to reason that Cheyenne might benefit from the same routine.

She took the child up to the bathroom and ran her a bath, listening for Marty, but he still hadn't come in. While Cheyenne bathed, Juliette bathed Bobby in a small tub in the sink, then fed him a bottle while the little girl dried and dressed. He was sound asleep by then, so she put him down for the night. After Cheyenne's bath her eyes were growing heavy-lidded but Juliette suspected she'd meet with mass resistance if she were to suggest bedtime. Instead, she asked Cheyenne if she could read her some stories.

She read two books, and by the time she got half-way through the second one, the little girl was fast asleep. Juliette eased her into bed and tucked the covers around her. As she did so, she heard the back door open, and Inky gave one small yip. She hesitated a moment, then went down to meet her husband.

Marty had icicles hanging from his hat, and his clothes were completely covered in white. He groaned as he eased off his gloves and cursed beneath his breath. She hurried forward and began unbuttoning his outer coat, knowing from watching him fumble at lunchtime that his fingers would be too numb to manage the buttons with any ease. He took off his hat and hung it up, then tossed everything else into the tub in the laundry room except for his coat. Juliette reached up and pulled off the balaclava that had protected his face, but when she looked up at him, the white patches around his eyes and nose alarmed her.

She bit back a protest. He'd been doing this long before he'd met her so he must know how far he could push his luck without actually doing any frost-bite damage. He leaned back against the wall and indicated his boots. "Could you…?"

She nodded. As he lifted one foot, she knelt and began to tug at it. To her surprise the first boot came off fairly easily. The second one was a little tougher, but finally it came off, too. Marty winced and hobbled a few steps. "My feet feel like two blocks of wood," he said.

Juliette eased her arm beneath his shoulder. "Will it help if you lean on me?"

He draped one arm heavily over her shoulder.

"Thanks." He looked around as they moved through the kitchen. "Where's Cheyenne? And the baby?"

Though the last was clearly an afterthought, she didn't call attention to it. "They're asleep. I waited dinner as long as I could, but I think it's important for both of them to have routines."

Marty grimaced. "I should have called and told you to go ahead. Sorry. We had a difficult birth with one of the older cows and I forgot what time it was."

Juliette couldn't prevent a smile. He hadn't deliberately decided not to call! "It's all right. But I'd appreciate the call in future if you can remember."

He glanced down at her as they moved through the house, and his face registered apprehension. "Did Cheyenne give you fits today?"

The feel of his long frame towering over her was doing funny things to her system, but she forced herself to pay attention to what he was saying. "No. We got along pretty well. She was a little testy before dinner but I think she was hungry."

He nodded, and she could almost feel the relief in his tone. "That's good." He didn't say anything more as they mounted the stairs, but when she made a move to leave at the bedroom door, he held on to her. "Come talk to me while I put on dry clothes."

She hesitated, but there was really no reason she could give for her reluctance. And she didn't really even know why she felt reluctant to start with. She was his wife now. So she went in with him and pulled her feet up to sit cross-legged on the bed while he got out fresh clothing. Inky leaped up and lay beside her and she held her breath, sure Marty would object, but if he even noticed the dog, he didn't say anything.

It felt odd, being in the bedroom with him, and the butterflies that his presence always inspired were alive and well in her stomach. He started to unbutton his shirt, but his fingers still weren't working easily. She slipped off the bed and walked to him. "Can I help?"

"Thanks." He dropped his arms and stood quietly as she lifted her hands to the top button and began to work her way down.

He was so much taller than she, even in his bare feet, that her eyes were nearly level with his shirt buttons. The butterflies flew up in a big cloud and started churning around in her stomach and her fingers fumbled with the buttons. She didn't dare look up at him and kept her eyes on her task. The room was silent except for their breathing.

Arousal and excitement formed a knot in her belly and her pulse suddenly was racing, rocketing through her body like a raft in a whitewater stretch of river. She took a deep breath, trying to settle her nerves, telling herself to stop acting like a silly virgin. All she was doing was helping her husband with a difficult task.

Her fingers traveled down over the buttons until she reached his belt. She hesitated for a moment, then set her hands on the buckle and opened it, slipping it free of his belt loops. His hands came up and he tugged the shirt free of his jeans. She unbuttoned the last few buttons, trying not to notice the hard male body beneath the layers of fabric.

His breathing seemed labored and harsh. Wordlessly he held up his forearms and she unbuttoned the cuffs. Then she stepped back as he shucked off the shirt. Beneath it he wore a navy-blue thermal shirt and he quickly tore that off over his head.

She took another step back, toward the door, as a primitive female vulnerability coursed through her and she forgot about being silly. The need to escape was overwhelming, but as she looked up into his blazing blue eyes, she froze. His gaze was hot as he looked down her body, lingering on the swell of her breasts and the vee at her thighs. He covered the distance between them in one stride, muttering, ''Juliette.''

''Marty, wait.''

But if he even heard her he gave no sign as his mouth came down on hers. Her palms landed solidly against the steely planes of his chest and as his lips settled on hers, she was aware of nothing but Marty's big body and the love that welled up inside her for this man, this husband about whom she needed to learn so much.

His mouth was warm and firm, demanding, slanting over hers while his arms came around her, pulling her into hot, sizzling contact with his hard frame. Juliette sighed into his mouth, an aching, needy whimper that caused his arms to draw her even closer. His tongue sought hers, and with no hesitation she gave him what he wanted, twining her arms around his neck and threading her fingers through his thick, gold-tipped curls, shaping his skull with small, restless fingers.

Marty shifted his grip on her, sliding one hand firmly down her back to cup her bottom. He changed the angle of his mouth, groaning as he pushed himself forward, spreading her legs wide with his big body and pressing himself firmly against her. "I want you," he panted. "Now."

She tore her mouth from his. "The door—"

And he was gone. In two strides he reached the door, then turned and pointed at Inky. "Out."

As soon as the dog was through the door, he shut and locked it, and in two more strides he was back with her, pulling her with him to the bed. He tore back the quilt and sheets, then turned to her again, his fingers shaking as his big hands moved gently over her body, tugging off her sweater and the turtleneck she wore beneath.

He stopped then, her shirt dropping from his fingers as his hungry gaze devoured her, and she suddenly felt as if there wasn't enough air in the room. She took a deep breath and his gaze was riveted to her breasts, covered only by a lacy blue bra.

He laughed, deep in his throat. "I might change my mind about the color blue." Then he raised his hands and cupped her shoulders, and she gasped at the icy feel of his fingers on her skin.

He pulled her against him again, breast to chest, and she no longer noticed the chill.

Then he took her hands and placed them at the button of his jeans. "Help me," he said. She did, unbuttoning and unzipping his pants. Then she unfastened her own while he was stepping out of his and removing his socks, doing the same with her own clothing.

When he looked up again, she heard the breath he sucked in, and she was suddenly, fiercely glad she'd worn the pretty matching thong that went with the bra.

He swallowed, and she watched the movement of his strong, tanned throat. "Juliette," he said hoarsely, "you're going to give me a heart attack." He put his still-cold hands on her hips and pulled her to him, and she gasped at both the cold and the intimacy as he slid his palms back and down over her naked buttocks. "Are these from your fancy store?"

She nodded, smiling as her lips touched his chest. He was the hardest man she'd ever met in every way there was. His arms bulged, and his back was roped with thick muscle on either side of the hollow of his spine. His chest was a solid sheet of unyielding man beneath the mat of dark curl, giving way to a flat, ridged stomach and firm, hairy thighs. He was, she thought with dreamy pleasure, every woman's imaginary lover.

And he was hers.

Was he ever. Beneath the white briefs he still wore, the outline of his arousal jutted against the fabric in a way that left her in no doubt about how he was feeling. He bent and lifted her effortlessly to the bed, but before he joined her, he hooked his thumbs in her tiny panties and stripped them down and off. "You'll have to unhook your bra," he said.

As she moved to comply, his hand settled possessively over the triangle of silvery curls between her legs. She gasped again at the coolness of his hand, but she didn't try to move away, lying motionless as his eyes roved up and down her body.

She remembered what Silver had said about his first wife, and she had a moment's sudden doubt. She was so small she didn't really even need a bra for support. Her hands came up almost automatically and crossed over her breasts, and Marty's eyes narrowed.

"Don't," he said. "I want to see all of you." Deliberately he removed his hand from her and took off his briefs in one smooth motion. He turned to the bedside table and withdrew a small packet from the drawer, fitting its contents over his thick length, and she gulped, her mouth dry and her pulse racing. He wanted her, there was no doubt of that. But if Rob had been quite so...impressive, her memory didn't recall it, and she moved restlessly, an uneasy fear taking root.

Marty read the expression on her face, and his arms came around her as he slid onto the bed and pulled her to him. She gasped as he pressed boldly into the soft mound of her belly. "Don't worry," he said. "It'll be all right."

"That's e-easy for you to say," she gasped, and he chuckled, pushing his hips against her. He rolled her beneath him, pressing wild, hot kisses to her face as he settled himself between her thighs. His whole big body was shaking with need, and his hands cruised over her, pebbling her nipples as the sensitive peaks responded to his stroking. She wrapped her arms as far around him as she could reach, stunned and overwhelmed by the *rightness* of the feel of him. She couldn't remember anything of Rob anymore, all she could think of was Marty, and she arched upward against him, silently pleading for his claiming.

He took her mouth again in a sure, strong kiss, thrusting his tongue deep and groaning when she responded in kind. His hand slid between them and a small part of her was amazed that he no longer felt chilled. Then his fingers slipped down into the soft folds of her body and she felt a single, hard finger probing. She whimpered, lifting herself against his hand and he pressed the butt of his palm against her as his finger slid deep within. He made small circles with his palm and she shook helplessly, a cry wrenched from her throat as the waves of pleasure rose over her and her body tensed with desire.

He withdrew his hand and she felt a sudden, intimate probe of blunt male flesh replacing it. He kept his mouth on hers as he moved his hips steadily forward, sliding easily into her for a moment. Then her body refused to admit him.

They both stopped moving, shocked and surprised.

"I...it's been a long time—" she got out.

"You had a baby. That changes things," he whispered against her mouth. "I'll try not to hurt you."

She gulped, clutching at his back as sensation ebbed and flowed within her. "I don't care. Do it *now.*"

He hesitated for a moment, rearing up to look down at her. Then, holding himself on his elbows above her, he kept her gaze ensnared by his as he shoved into her, pressing on.

She gasped and turned her face into his shoulder.

Marty shuddered. "You're so tight—" He stopped speaking, and his hips plunged into her, measuring himself again and then again. With each movement he rubbed against her, igniting the sensual fires that coiled within her belly. "Mine," he muttered. "My angel..." His body moved harder and faster; he reached down and pulled her thighs up, and she wrapped her legs around his waist, whimpering as he doubled his cadence. She strained against him, loving his primitive claiming, feeling the rising surge of undeniable pleasure—and then her body broke free of her control and she arched beneath him, her body tightening repeatedly as she found release. A shiver worked its way up Marty's spine, and he groaned as her fingers clutched at him. Then he stiffened above her, his hips pumping relentlessly until the power of his climax slowly, gradually decreased and he gave a final groan and collapsed. He rolled over immediately, taking her with him so that she lay over him like a blanket, her legs draped around his hips, her arms around his neck. After a moment, his hands stroked up and down her spine.

And then he chuckled.

"What's so funny?" She yawned. She could go right to sleep, just like the kids.

"I'm not cold anymore," he told her. "I'll have to remember this. You're better than an electric blanket."

"Thanks, I think," she said. She felt relaxed and easy with him, though a part of her yearned for intimate conversation and whispered words of love. Those wouldn't be forthcoming, though, she knew, her spirits sinking. She was a warm body to him, a mother-housekeeper-bedwarmer all rolled into one convenient, easy-to-use package.

The air in the room suddenly seemed cooler, and she shivered. Marty reached down and flipped the blankets over them both. His hands continued to rove idly over her back and bottom, but the pleasure was gone and she lay on him, her heart heavy.

"Are you all right?" His voice was hesitant. "You're so little and delicate and I'm—"

"I'm fine."

Without warning he rolled again, pinning her beneath him. He held her face in his hands when she would have turned it away, and she closed her eyes to avoid his probing gaze. "What's wrong?"

"Nothing." *Other than the fact that I love you.*

"Open your eyes."

She did, reluctantly. She'd have to remember to be careful in the future. He was surprisingly tuned in to her moods.

"Juliette…" He hesitated. "I—"

A sound floated into the room…a crying baby. Bobby. He wasn't really wailing yet, but she knew he was awake and lonely. Immediately she stiffened, beginning to slide off him, but he held her in place despite her struggles.

"Where are you going?"

"Bobby's awake," she said. "He'll be hungry after his nap."

Marty's grip didn't relax for a long moment, and she had a sudden, ridiculous fear that he wasn't going to let her go to her child. Then he withdrew his hands, letting her scramble from the warmth of their lovemaking. "Then go."

His voice was almost sulky, like a child's, and she said, "What were you going to say?"

"Nothing." He sat up and ran his hands through his hair and his fingers clenched against his scalp as Bobby's fussing increased in volume. "Would you just go shut that baby up?"

"Marty, he's a *baby*. He doesn't understand—"

"I said go, didn't I?" His voice was irritable now. "I'm not trying to stop you."

She hurriedly dressed without speaking again, fighting tears. Then she remembered dinner. "I have a plate in the oven for you," she informed him, casting him a single glance as she left the room.

Part of her wanted to scream at his seeming callousness, but she couldn't bring herself to do it. Marty was a good man. His actions around her son only proved how deeply he was hurting. Would this ever get easier for him? She'd do anything in the world to help him past it, except give up Bobby.

And that, she thought, with a sudden, sickening flash of intuition, was probably the one thing she could do that would ease the strain that continually crept back in between them.

If he'd known that she came with a baby, he would never have married her.

But even as he had the thought, Marty knew it wasn't true. He would probably do it all over again even if she'd had two babies, because he wanted her so badly. Even now, still lying where he'd taken her, he was ready again just thinking about her tiny, perfectly made body, her rosy nipples and delicate mound of blond curls, the surprising strength in the slim legs that had twined about his waist and drawn him deeper into her—

He cursed and rolled out of the bed, stalking across the room to the bathroom, erect and aching. What in hell was he going to do?

He showered, his mood still dark, dressed and went downstairs to eat. Juliette was in the kitchen already.

She had a warm dinner ready for him and he grunted his thanks. The kid was in his little seat on the counter again, and though Juliette had tactfully turned the cradle away, he could see an occasional little hand or foot flailing in the air as the kid wriggled and squirmed. He couldn't force himself to ignore the baby, sneaking glances over at the seat repeatedly. Every now and then the kid would coo or squeal and Marty couldn't help flinching at the small sounds.

The instant he was done, he took his dishes to the sink and then turned away from the kitchen. "I'll be in the office."

As he walked through the living room, he had to step over toys and games spread across the floor. Inky lay on the couch in the middle of an afghan as if he owned it. The house had never looked like this when Lora was alive and he'd done his best—which admittedly was pretty pathetic—after she'd died to keep it picked up. He'd expected things to be better after Juliette arrived.

Then he realized Juliette had come to stand behind him. "She's precious," she said, and he realized she was talking about Cheyenne. "And very, very bright. I'm finding that the best way to keep her out of trouble is to keep her busy."

"This place is a wreck," he said, completely ignoring her words. He pointed to the child-induced chaos in the living room. "I married you to fix this, not make it worse."

Her face lost every ounce of the pretty color it had held since she'd come downstairs. Her eyes were huge and dark, and he could see the hurt in their depths.

He felt small and mean, and he put a hand on her arm. "I'm sorry," he said belatedly. "I didn't mean that the way it sounded."

She raised her eyebrows, and when her eyes met his again, there was absolutely no expression that he could read. She didn't say a word, simply pulled her arm from beneath his hand, then knelt and began picking up the pieces of a game, ignoring him until he walked on into the office.

It wasn't until he came back into the kitchen for more coffee that he noticed something was different. And then he realized what it was. The kitchen was spotless. The curtains and rugs were clean; the counters held nothing but the normal things that were kept on them unless you counted the baby seat; the cupboards and refrigerator actually had space to set items in empty spots; and the floor had lost its dingy gray tone and actually shone.

"Wow," he said. "I didn't notice this before. You must have worked in here all day."

"I didn't neglect your daughter," she said, and he realized she was still mad at him for his tactless comments earlier.

"I didn't think you would," he said.

Juliette didn't answer him and there was an awkward silence for a moment. Then she spoke again, but it wasn't the personal conversation he wanted.

"May I use the phone?"

"Of course. This is your home."

"It's a long-distance call."

"That doesn't matter. Unless you're planning to spend hours on the phone to Japan every day, I don't have a problem with you making the calls you need to make.'' He was dying to know who she was calling. It drove him crazy that he knew so little about her he didn't even know who she cared enough about to place a long-distance call to, but he went into the living room and turned on the news to give her a little privacy.

She didn't say anything else, just picked up the handset. He could see her from his seat in the recliner as she punched in a number and waited for it to ring. He reached for the remote and turned the television down a few increments.

''Hello, Millicent. This is Juliette.'' He wondered if Juliette realized she'd grimaced when this Millicent person picked up on her end. Hmm, not on Juliette's list of favorite people, apparently. So why would she call her?

Whoever Millicent was, she must have had plenty to say. Juliette listened, nodding or shaking her head, for several long minutes before she opened her mouth. ''I'm not coming back to California, Millicent. This week I married a man who lives in South Dakota.''

She held the phone away from her ear at the response, then spoke again. ''He's a widowed rancher with a young daughter, and he's very well able to support Bobby and me. Don't worry, I'll still bring Bobby to visit and of course, when he's older, he can come and stay with you for vacations.''

Juliette was frowning now. ''I'm sorry, that's not possible. We don't have room here for visitors.''

A blatant lie, if he'd ever heard one. He knew she had the kid sleeping in the room that had been

Deck's, but there was a perfectly good king-size bed in there.

"Perhaps in a month or two," she was saying. "I want to get settled into my new home before I go running off." She listened again. "No! It doesn't matter what you do. This marriage is legal, and this is my family and Bobby's now. I would never exclude you from his life, but we're not coming back to live with you. Our life is here now."

He didn't realize he was on his feet until she hung up the telephone and he stood in front of her. "What the hell was that all about?"

Juliette looked totally drained.

He put his hands on her shoulders and began to gently massage. The answers to the questions that had rolled around in his head were right here in front of him, he was sure of it.

"That was my mother-in-law," she said, apparently forgetting that she'd been mad at him before the phone rang. "My first mother-in-law. Bobby's grandmother. She's...not very happy with me."

"Did she threaten you?" His voice was hard. Nobody was going to intimidate his wife.

"She didn't really mean it as a threat," Juliette said. 'Well, maybe she did, but only because she's so upset. My husband and I lived with her. After Rob died, she took over, made all the decisions. I was pregnant and alone and she seemed so kind. And she is, deep down. We both missed Rob and we shared that. Then Bobby was born. She was thrilled." Juliette sighed, and he rubbed at the taut cords in her neck. "Millicent—that's her name—isn't shy about making her opinions known. And she had an opinion on everything I did with my son. It created a strain between us. I felt that she wanted to replace Rob with Bobby, and I wasn't going to let that happen. She nearly smothered Rob. In fact, he married me without telling her, or she'd probably have objected to that.''

''Sounds like a control freak,'' he commented.

''Yes, but I pity her,'' Juliette said. ''Her husband left her when Rob was in elementary school. Then Rob died when he was only twenty-eight of a previously undiagnosed heart condition. She was devastated. I can't blame her for wanting to keep Bobby close.''

''So that's why you were so eager to marry me. I'd wondered.'' He didn't stop massaging her neck, but Juliette slid off the stool on which she'd been sitting and walked around to the other side of the counter, moving away from his touch.

''She has a great deal of money,'' she said defensively. ''She got me fired from one job, and she wouldn't hesitate to do anything she could to force me to move back home.''

Good God. It sounded so melodramatic, but Juliette certainly believed it. ''What else did she do?''

''Nothing. But she implied in one telephone conversation that she would have me declared an unfit mother if I didn't come back. I think she might have tried it, too.'' She looked at him, and her eyes were defeated. ''That's when I saw your ad. I couldn't take the chance that you wouldn't want to marry me if I told you about Bobby.''

So that was it. That was the piece of the puzzle he hadn't understood until now.

"We need to talk," he said. "Why don't we go to bed?"

She stared at him for a moment, one hand coming up to her throat in a curiously defensive gesture. Then she nodded and went back into the kitchen. When she came back, she had the baby.

"I'll let the dog out," he said, turning away fast.

Six

Her hands were trembling as she pulled back the covers and got into bed. Marty slid in on the other side, snapping off the lamp on the bedside table before drawing the covers over them and lying back.

For a long moment there was silence in the bedroom. It wasn't a comfortable one. She half expected him to reach for her, to pull her beneath him and make her forget the reasons she felt like crying.

But he didn't.

After what seemed like a long, long time, Marty cleared his throat. "I wish it could be different," he said. "I wish I could love your son. But all I can see...when he cries, the memories—" in the dark she could hear his voice break "—I just can't take it."

"Sh-h-h." She reacted instinctively, shocked by the depths of despair she heard. She reached for his hand beneath the covers and stroked it gently, trying not to cry out when he clasped her smaller palm in a death grip that hurt. "It's all right." She took a deep breath, rolling onto her side and resting her free hand on his broad chest, over his heart. "Marty, I don't want to cause you pain. Please believe that. If I'd known, I'd never have married—"

"That's what I was afraid of," he said.

They both were silent again, contemplating thoughts neither wished to voice.

"I'll have to leave," she said finally. "There's no other way." The words fell between them, hushed and deadly, and her heart broke at the thought of going away, of never seeing Marty again, never stroking his tousled curls or knowing the incredible splendor of his lovemaking.

"No." In contrast his voice was loud. Harsh. "I want you to stay. Cheyenne needs you now." But she noticed he didn't say *he* needed her, or that he loved her.

She hesitated.

"You can keep him away from me," Marty said. "As long as I don't have to see him, or hear him…"

She knew it was impossible, ridiculous. But she didn't say so. Now, while Bobby was an infant, the idea might work. But he was going to grow rapidly, stay awake longer, talk, crawl, walk. Did Marty know what he was saying?

He must. He'd been around during Cheyenne's infancy. He knew how toddlers and preschoolers were. There would be no hiding a growing child. And what would happen when they had more children?

Maybe by then the grief and pain that seemed to

be eating at Marty from the inside out would be dulled, blunted. Maybe by then he would love her the way she loved him.

Maybe time was the answer. Maybe if she simply accepted what he could give her for now and waited for time to heal the wounds that scarred his heart, maybe one day he'd be able to be a father to all the children they had—his, hers and theirs.

"Please," he said, and she realized she'd let the silence run on unanswered. "Please don't leave me, angel." He moved then, pulling her into his arms and cuddling her against his big body. "I've just found you, and I don't want to lose what we have."

The words melted away her reservations. They weren't words of love, but they were close enough to ensnare her, close enough to bring the love she felt for him surging to the surface, sweeping away the doubts and fear that plagued her.

"I won't leave you," she whispered. She stretched up her head so that she could brush a kiss against his jaw, and he rolled, pushing her to her back and settling himself between her thighs. She made a humming sound of pleasure as his hard flesh securely pushed into the cradle where her legs met, and he braced himself on his arms above her.

"I want to make love to my wife," he said in a deep, rough voice.

The next few weeks were busy. She did her best to switch Bobby's schedule around so that he was sleeping much of the limited time Marty was in the house, and she was aware that Marty kept a rigid schedule as well. Probably far more so than normal.

Still, it seemed to work, and she took heart. *Time will heal,* she repeated to herself over and over.

It snowed heavily several times, and the roads were closed, keeping her housebound, but she talked to both Silver and Lyn on the telephone, and she barely minded the enforced solitude. She began teaching Cheyenne to print her name and then the alphabet. During nap times she scoured the Internet for early-childhood education and child-rearing information, and she ordered several educational books through an on-line service. Marty teased her when they arrived, but she noticed he was reading them, too, in the evenings. Cheyenne threw fits from time to time, and Juliette began to take her cues from Marty, sending the little girl to her room until she calmed. Cheyenne's histrionics fascinated Bobby. His little eyes went wide, and his mouth was a slack *O* of permanent surprise that made Juliette laugh.

She got more and more comfortable in the house, rearranging furniture, drawers and cupboards and making lists of changes she wanted to make, then discussing them with Marty. He generally had little objection, and when the weather warmed up so that she could open up the house, she planned to paint the cabinets in the kitchen and utility room.

She took the children over to visit Silver one day in late January when the weather broke. Lyn came over, as well, and under her more knowledgeable eye, the women pored over seed and plant catalogs in anticipation of spring. Silver was due anytime, and Deck had forbidden her to set foot outside the door for fear she'd slip on the icy, frozen ground.

"So how are things?" Lyn's green eyes were concerned as she eyed Juliette over a cup of herbal tea.

Juliette hesitated. "It depends on what time it is when you ask me that." She looked at both of her new friends, so obviously concerned for her situation, and she sighed. "Marty ignores Bobby. We talked about it once, and it was so hard for him—" She stopped as her throat grew tight with tears.

"Oh, honey." Silver put a hand over hers. "Give him time."

"That's what I keep telling myself," she said. "But I don't know if he'll ever adjust to having another little boy in his home. I told him I would go…" The tears welled up and flowed over, and Lyn got up to bring a box of tissues to the table.

"You love him, don't you?" she asked quietly as she resumed her seat.

Juliette blew her nose and worked up a trembling smile. "Is it that obvious?"

"Only to other women who are wild about bullheaded ranchers," Silver said. "Does he know?"

Juliette shook her head. "We made a basic business arrangement. Love wasn't a part of it."

"Wait a minute." Lyn shook her head. "I saw the way he kissed you. You can't tell me he doesn't have some feelings for you"

Juliette grimaced. "Only below the belt."

All three women laughed. But when the sounds died away, Silver said, "What did he say when you told him you would leave if he wanted you to?"

"He said he didn't want me to go." It was comforting to hear the words spoken aloud. "He said…he said he didn't want to lose what we had just found."

"Hmm." The sound was noncommittal, but the satisfied smile that lifted Silver's brow and the knowing look she sent Lyn said she was pleased. "Give him time," was all she said.

When Juliette went home, she was loaded with catalogs and Silver's favorite recipe for shepherd's pie. She loved to cook and bake, a half-forgotten skill she'd neglected, and she delighted in feeding Marty, who was appreciative of every effort. She had caught him boasting to his brother about her cooking one day last week, telling Deck he was going to have to starting watching how much he ate.

After the children were in bed, they made love as they did nearly every night. She wondered if she'd ever be able to tell Marty how much she cherished those moments when he reached for her. Later, passion sated, she slept in the curve of his arm, cuddled against him throughout the long, cold winter night.

But the dark hours of night weren't the only times he demonstrated his need for her. He came in sometimes in the afternoons, when he thought there was a chance that both children would be napping. He dragged her into the bathroom off the utility room for one memorable shower, and once they even made love in the pantry, when he caught her rummaging through mismatched canning jars.

He yanked the door firmly shut and took her from behind, his body hot against her back and his breath harsh in her ear as she braced herself against the shelves in the narrow aisle. He caught her chin and tugged her face back to his, claiming her mouth in a deep, wild kiss. She reached back, palmed his smooth, taut buttocks, pulling him deeper into her, and he groaned, sliding one hand around to her belly to hold her to him. He slid one finger down into the nest of curls protecting her delicate femininity, seeking out the little swollen nub of her desire, his rhythmic strokes pushing her body back and forth against his finger, and she quickly climaxed, convulsing around him, triggering his own shuddering, pounding finish. When it was over, she could feel his legs trembling as he slumped over her, panting, and they both laughed.

"Deck'll think I'm going lame," he said, chuckling as he gasped for breath.

"Ha. He'll know exactly what we've been doing," she predicted darkly. "I'll never be able to look him in the eye again."

It wasn't until later that she realized they hadn't thought of protection that afternoon, and she wondered if Marty even thought of the risk they'd taken.

Of all the things that had gone wrong in those first few days, the loss of his laughter had been what she'd missed the most. Marty seemed a happy man, whistling his way through the parking lot that first night, gently teasing her during their long phone conversations until they both had been laughing.

Now the whistling resumed and throughout the early days in the month of February, the man she'd met in Rapid City returned. He began to sing in the shower. His dimples winked in his cheeks, his white teeth flashed in frequent smiles, and his blue eyes held a merry devilish gleam when he was up to some trick.

And she fell deeper and deeper in love.

Only two things marred her growing contentment.

The first was her former mother-in-law. Millicent called the ranch at least twice a week, demanding that Juliette return to California with Bobby, that she send the child to California to be raised ''properly'' because Lord only knew what he'd learn growing up around a bunch of cowboys, demanding that Juliette prepare a guest room and set a date for her to visit.

On an evening in the second week of February, Marty came in late in the evening from a bad premature birth in which the cow's stomach had ruptured while he and two of the hired hands were trying to help her deliver a breech calf. The calf lived but the cow died an hour later, and he had to send the baby over to Cal's to a cow that had lost her calf. The only good news, he told Juliette in disgust, was that the cow had accepted the substitute calf.

She helped him out of his stiff, soaking clothing. The outer layers were covered with blood and gore that she was reluctant to examine too closely as she shoved them into the washing machine. She turned to see that Marty had stripped off every stitch of clothing. His body was sculpted with layer upon layer of hard-earned muscle and her breathing began to come faster as she surveyed the broad sweep of his shoulders, the firm muscled contours of his chest and abdomen and the way the mat of hair across his chest narrowed to a thin line down past his navel, then blossomed again in a luxuriant tangle of curl at his thighs. His legs were as solid as oak trees…and that wasn't the only thing that was solid, she thought in amusement, her gaze sliding back up to his face.

His eyes were a hot, blazing blue; she knew that look. Whenever Marty turned that look on her, her bones seemed to turn to gelatin and her lower belly quivered in anticipation.

He covered the small distance between them, standing so close that his erection brushed her belly. "Are the kids in bed?"

She nodded, swallowing, not sure her voice would work.

"Good," he muttered as his arms came around her and pulled her hard against him. "Kiss me."

She did, turning her face up and sliding her arms around his neck as he fumbled between them with her shirt buttons. His tongue invaded her mouth with familiar sweetness and she met him with her own response, her body singing as he tore open her shirt and thrust his hands inside to cover her breasts, rubbing the nipples to taut points beneath her bra.

Then he stroked his palms down, across the satiny skin of her torso to the belt and the snap of the new jeans she'd bought just weeks ago, stripping them from her with such efficiency that she barely had time to register the cooler air on her body. "Brr, it's cold in here," she managed in between kisses.

Marty lifted his head and grinned, a cocky masculine expression. "Couldn't prove it by me."

She burst out laughing as he picked her up, stopping only to grab a small foil packet from the pocket of his jeans.

"What's that?" she teased. "Your rabbit's foot that you carry everywhere?"

He grinned as he dropped his head and gently closed his teeth on her neck. "I've learned to be prepared for anything when you're around." Leaving her outer clothing strewn across the utility room floor, he carried her into the relative warmth of the kitchen. But as she slid down his body, his laughter died away and he bent to her once more. "I can't get enough of you," he muttered, sliding his mouth along her jaw. "It's damned embarrassing. Deck's caught me day-dreaming a dozen times." He pressed a strand of stinging kisses to her collarbone and cruised on down across her breastbone to the slight swell of one breast, boldly brushing aside her bra, taking the tip into his mouth and suckling with hard purpose. She cried out as arrows of intense pleasure streaked straight to her womb, and she wriggled her hips against him, wordlessly begging for his possession.

He lifted his head and gazed down over her body, his eyes searing a path. "I spend hours every day wondering what kind of underwear you've got on."

Today she was wearing black lace, a pretty push-up bra that made the most of her insignificant cleavage, and high, French-cut panties, and she was thankful again for her brief sojourn in lingerie sales. Marty loved her underwear—he'd even gotten her a camisole in deep-wine-red during a trip to the mall last weekend, and she'd worn it the very same evening. For a few minutes.

Now she twisted her arm behind her back and unhooked the bra, tossing it aside as he donned protection. Marty looked up and smiled as he caught her watching him, but there was a feral quality to the expression. He caught her by the hips and dragged her against him, burning her flesh with the heat consuming him, guiding her back and forth in a twisting motion that brushed her breasts against his ridged stomach. He was so much larger than she was that sometimes she felt like a doll in his arms. As he bent his head and sought her lips again, he pushed her head back against the muscled power of his arm. As he devoured her, she felt his other hand slip down her belly, sliding beneath the edge of her panties and probing the soft curls at the apex of her thighs, curving down between her legs to the slippery cleft where she pulsed with heat and need.

"Ah," he crooned against her mouth. "You're so wet for me. So wet..."

She felt him tugging the leg of her panties aside as he lifted her with his other arm, pressing himself against her, and without even removing the panties, his blunt column of searing man flesh slid securely into the snug channel of her body.

They both groaned. She lifted her legs and linked them around his hips, and he briefly closed his eyes as he growled, "I love it when you do that."

She wrapped her arms around his strong neck, clinging to him as he began to thrust. Her body quivered beneath his powerful motions, swelling waves of desire pushing her higher and higher for long moments until she hung suspended at the peak for one breathless instant. Then her body began to convulse, drawing her taut in repeated spasms in his arms, and he made a low sound in his throat, holding himself perfectly still as her flesh squeezed his in the ultimate intimacy. When she finally lay limp and panting against his chest, he began to move again, thrusting in and out of her in great surging motions, gripping her hips and sliding her up and down, taking her into a second maelstrom of sexual urgency, firing her response again until she climaxed again at the same instant he did. His teeth were gritted, the cords in his neck stood out in rigid detail, and he locked her to him with steely arms until they both were still.

There was no sound in the kitchen for a long, laden moment. She expected him to set her on her feet, and she was mildly shocked when he simply wrapped a brawny arm beneath her bottom again and began to walk toward the stairs.

"Marty!" She began to protest, but he stopped her words with a hard kiss.

When he lifted his head, she could do nothing more than offer him a dreamy smile. "Whatever you say, O master."

He grinned. "I say we head for bed." He rolled his hips against her once, his still-taut length drawing a surprising pulse of response from her.

But as he set a foot on the bottom step, the telephone rang. He stopped. Swore. Retraced his path to the kitchen, still carrying her.

"This better be good," he muttered as he reached for the phone. "Or I'm going to kill whoever's on the other end... Lucky Stryke," he said into the handset.

Juliette couldn't hear the speaker, but she watched as his brows snapped together and his face grew grim. "She's not available. Can I take a message?" Apparently, the speaker had plenty to say because he listened silently for a long, tense moment. Finally he spoke again. "Listen, lady, Juliette will not ever give in to your bully behavior. She and Bobby belong here now. If she wants to invite you to visit, that's her decision and we'll make you welcome. But if you call here *one more time* with that attitude, I'm going to be filing harassment charges against you to prohibit you from calling or visiting at all. *Is that clear?*"

Juliette listened in stunned silence as she realized the caller must be her former mother-in-law, Millicent. Her heart gave a small leap of pleasure when he spoke Bobby's name. It was the first time since... since *ever* that she'd heard him call her child anything other than "he" or "the kid." Her heart warmed even more at the way he defended her, and she wondered if Millicent was smart enough to heed his warning.

When he slapped the handset back on its cradle, her mind was still reeling. But Marty acted as if nothing had happened. "Now," he said. "I believe we were heading for the bedroom...?"

The other flaw in the growing perfection of her life was Marty's continued avoidance of her son. Throughout the early weeks of the new year and her new marriage, he had studiously steered clear of any chance that he might have to come face-to-face with Bobby.

He'd defended her son against Millicent's aggressive tactics, though Juliette feared his outspoken attitude might lead to costly legal repercussions. Since that day, she'd hoped even more strongly that Marty would accept her son, but he didn't appear to be any closer to doing so than he had been the day they'd arrived.

But one night toward the end of February, something happened to give her hope again. She was bathing Cheyenne when Marty came in from the barn.

She heard him come in, earlier than usual, and she

called out, "Hi. We're almost done up here. There's a plate in the oven for you."

She finished bathing Cheyenne quickly, as anxious as the little girl to see Marty, but as she was toweling dry Cheyenne's hair, she heard his footsteps on the stairs. Before she knew it, he was in the bathroom with them, kissing her hello and kneeling to hug his daughter. Then he froze.

Bobby was in his little seat where he usually stayed during Cheyenne's bath. He was fed and dry and happy as a fat little lamb, kicking his tiny feet and waving his arms in a vain and uncoordinated effort to touch one of the toys hanging from the crossbar above him.

Marty's position put him almost directly in front of the baby. He couldn't fail to see him, and Juliette froze, as well. She expected him to bolt from the room but he didn't.

Cheyenne giggled and pointed to her stepbrother. "Look, Daddy, Bobby's trying to grab that."

Slowly Marty nodded. He looked at the infant. "I see." Then he reached out and touched a tentative finger to Bobby's small, stockinged foot. "It's hard to believe you were ever that small," he said to Cheyenne.

Juliette's heart skipped a beat. She had to stop herself from reaching out to hug him. Instead, as he rose to his feet and casually took his daughter's hand, she forced herself to act normally, as if nothing out of the ordinary had happened. She lifted Bobby and carried him down with her, making his bottle and feeding him before putting him down for the night, just as she always did. But her heart was singing.

The lingering tension in the house began to ease even more in the last week of the month. Marty stopped on his way through the kitchen one day and lifted the infant seat from the counter, positioning it facing the room instead of the wall. "He must be getting tired of that wallpaper," was all he said, but she took it as a sign that the sight of the baby no longer hurt his heart as it once had.

And her heart swelled with hope.

One morning Marty brought in an ice-covered early calf found shivering beside its mother, who'd calved out on a hillside. It wasn't moving much at all. It had been only twenty degrees this morning and who know how long the poor little thing had been lying out there? Marty brought the baby into the utility room and set it in a tub of warm water in the utility room.

The baby, a little bull, recovered quickly as he warmed up and by the time Juliette and Cheyenne had him dried off, they both were soaked. When Marty came back to check him later, the calf was charging around the utility room bawling for mama and Juliette was laughing herself silly as Cheyenne sat on top of the dryer and watched her try to calm the little bull.

The phone rang, and she absently walked into the kitchen. "Hello?"

"My water broke. We're on our way to the hospital!" It was Silver. Her due date had come and gone, and she'd been planning to go to stay in Rapid City tomorrow until the baby was born, because another storm was predicted.

Juliette jumped up and down. "Oh, good luck!" Then she remembered what labor and delivery was like, and she chuckled. "You're going to need it."

"Thanks." Silver's voice was wry. "My contractions are still pretty mild and not frequent at all, but Deck isn't taking any chances. I figure he'll get me there in plenty of time to pace around for hours and hours."

When she hung up the phone, she turned to Marty, excitement dancing a fast jig in her stomach. "Silver's in labor. With a little luck, things'll go fast and you'll have a new niece or nephew tonight." She smiled at Marty, but her smile died half-born as she caught sight of the look on his face.

Without a word he wheeled and left the house, and she watched through the window as he strode along the shoveled path to the barn and disappeared inside.

Her heart, always tender and easily bruised where he was concerned, felt as thought it might shatter and fall right out of her chest. Though he still avoided Bobby, he didn't completely ignore the infant, and he hadn't seemed as tense and upset recently. A fragile hope had begun to take root within her, a hope that eventually he'd be able to accept her son.

But seeing his reaction to the news of his own brother's child's imminent arrival, she was forced to acknowledge that she'd been deluding herself, donning rose-colored glasses and refusing to see the grimmer, darker shades of his inability to open himself up to a baby again.

The knowledge was doubly troubling. She'd been silently eyeing her calendar for almost two weeks now. She'd missed her period in the middle of February, but she'd ignored it, telling herself it was just the strain of her new life. Right. It *did* have something to do with her new life, but she was afraid it wasn't just strain. It was one big virile hunk named Marty Stryker.

She knew when it had happened, too, and every time she walked into the pantry she shivered with pleasure at the memory of that wild, hot lovemaking. The time Marty had made love to her in the little room replayed itself again and again in her mind. Only now the delight she'd taken in the memory was tinged with distress. If she was pregnant, Marty would never be able to deal with it. What would she do?

He couldn't shake the terrible fear that gripped him as the hours crept by. It was—he glanced at the clock on the wall of the barn—almost four o'clock, and Silver had been in labor for half a day now. He wasn't normally a praying man, but he prayed now. Prayed that nothing would happen to her, that she'd survive this ordeal. Deck needed her so badly.

And the whole time, he fought images of Lora, soaking the seat of his truck with her blood as he frantically drove toward Rapid City.

He knew he should go into the house, knew he wasn't being fair, that Juliette was probably worried sick about him, but he couldn't bring himself to move. Finally, when the light faded from the winter sky, he forced himself to leave the sanctuary of the barn.

He steeled himself as he opened the back door, a frightening feeling of helplessness crashing over him. Lora had needed help that he couldn't give, and she'd died. Childbearing was a risky business, as he knew from the work he did every day. If something happened to Silver, his brother might not survive it.

Juliette was in the kitchen. She didn't look up or speak, and the dread in his chest congealed into a hard knot of fear. "Have...have you heard anything?" he croaked.

She looked up. Smiled. "You have a niece," she said. "At two-twenty this afternoon."

He could barely get the question out. "And... Silver?"

"Smug." Juliette laughed. "Labor was a breeze and she'd do it again tomorrow." She rolled her eyes. "My labor with Bobby was short but my memory is vivid. No way would I volunteer to do that again right away—" She stopped abruptly. "I'm going to the hospital tonight. Lyn's coming over to take care of the children."

Relief so intense it actually hurt was sweeping through him, and he sat down at the kitchen table before his legs gave out. "Thank God," he muttered. Then, as it really began to hit him that Silver was all right, he smiled back at Juliette. "Think I'll go with you," he said.

They drove to the hospital after a quick dinner, leaving the kids in Lyn's capable hands.

Parking in the lot outside the hospital, Marty was struck by a wave of memories, but he shoved them back. Things had gone right, for once, and he wasn't about to miss a chance to visit a hospital for a happy occasion.

They took the elevator to the birthing unit and found Silver's room. Marty took a deep breath. He could do this. He could. He saw the edge of the rolling bassinet around the corner of the partially drawn curtain, and just then he felt Juliette slide her small hand into his and squeeze.

He turned his head and looked down into her wide blue eyes, saw the compassion there and lifted her fingers to his lips. "Thank you."

And then the edge of the curtain was lifted aside, and Deck was grinning at them. "Hey! Hi! Come on in and meet the newest member of the family." His eyes telegraphed a concern that was at odds with his exuberant tone, but when Marty smiled at him, the tension in his face eased.

"So where's this beautiful girl?" Marty asked.

From behind the curtain, Silver's voice said, "Right here." Then she laughed. "Oh, you don't mean me!"

They entered the cubicle as Deck stepped to his wife's side and leaned over to place a tender kiss on her lips. If Marty hadn't been such a tough guy, the sight just might have made him bawl a little. It was so good to see Deck smile, to see joy replace the dark ache in his eyes that had mirrored his soul's sorrow for so many years after his twin had died.

Deck straightened from the kiss, still looking at his wife. "You'll always be beautiful to me," he said.

The open love in his tone made Marty a little uncomfortable. Again he was reminded of how his life had changed since Cheyenne's birth, when he'd stood in this hospital with the woman he loved.

Now he stood here with another wife beside him. One he'd married for far more practical reasons than love, one he desired so strongly that he could no longer imagine his life without her.

"And this," Deck said, indicating the bundle cuddled in the curve of Silver's arm, "is the other beauty in our family. Erica Silver Stryker, meet your aunt and uncle."

Juliette stepped forward, blocking Marty's view of the infant as Silver slipped the blanket back. "Well, hello, you little doll," she said inspecting the baby. She straightened and there were tears in her eyes. "She's perfect," she said. "Just perfect."

Curious, Marty stepped around her for a better view. The baby was *tiny*. Erica made Bobby seem enormous and full-grown, though there was actually less than half a year between their birthdates. She had a fuzzy cap of dark curls, and when she opened her eyes and looked around with the peculiar myopic stare that newborns possessed, he could see a distinctive ring of silver in each of the dark-blue irises.

"You're going to be as gorgeous as your mama," he told his new niece. "And it's a good thing, since your daddy's as homely as a cow chip."

He stroked a finger along her downy cheek and laughed when her little mouth automatically began rooting around, thinking a meal was on the way. "You're really something, little gal."

He straightened up, still grinning. Deck and Juliette were both staring at him with identical incredulous expressions.

"What?" he asked.

"Ah, nothing," said Deck hastily. "Nothing."

But he knew. They'd been waiting for his reaction. It struck him suddenly that the reason Juliette had stepped in front of him was to spare him having to look at the baby.

He put an arm around her shoulders and caressed

her neck with his thumb, silently telling her how much he appreciated her. "I guess you're going to want all the details now," was all he said to her.

"You bet." She held out her arms to Silver. "And I want to get my hands on that baby."

They left the women to talk baby stuff for a few minutes and walked out into the hallway. Marty playfully punched Deck in the arm. "You're doing good, little bro."

The brothers' eyes met.

"It still makes me sad," Deck said, "but I've finally moved on. Have you?"

Marty knew he wasn't referring to the death of their sister, but of his wife and son, and he knew he couldn't confront the images that waited. He'd conquered a lot of things, but… Carefully, he shrugged his shoulders. "More or less."

Deck's eyes narrowed. "Less." He slung an arm around Marty's shoulders as they walked back down the hall toward Silver's room. "I'm here if you need me."

The simple words clogged Marty's throat, and for a moment he couldn't answer. "Thanks," he finally managed. "But I'm okay."

Seven

On the first of March, a foot of snow fell. Highways and businesses were closed, but Marty and Deck still had to go out to feed the cattle they'd brought to the corral yesterday. All the cows ran into the corral to eat as the men pitched out the hay, and in the melee several calves got separated from their mothers and left behind.

Juliette had taken Cheyenne out to build a snowman while Bobby took his morning nap, and they watched as Marty and his brother chased down the group of calves that took off toward the creek. One, alone and panicked, ran the other way.

Juliette called out, then realized that the men wouldn't be able to hear her and certainly wouldn't be able to leave the calves they were collecting. She looked at Cheyenne. "I have to get that calf, honey.

Can you go back in the house and take off your wet things? I'll be in as soon as I catch him.''

Cheyenne didn't argue for once. As Juliette took off toward the gate, Cheyenne shouted after her, ''Get a rope from the barn!''

Juliette stopped in her tracks, wheeled and ran to the barn to collect the rope before following the calf's tracks up the hill and away from the house. She shook her head ruefully. A four-year-old who'd grown up out here knew more about handling cattle than she did. Sad state of affairs.

She couldn't even ride. Never having been around horses or cows in her entire life, the large creatures made her nervous. But she'd asked Marty to teach her to ride in the summer when calving and branding was finished. If she was going to live out here, she was going to have to learn to help outside. Marty didn't seem to expect it, and though he talked to her frequently about what he did during the day, he had never invited her to come out and help. Maybe he thought she didn't want to.

She was breathing hard when she finally slogged through the deep snow to the top of the hill. It was in the midtwenties, not terribly cold, and she was sweating inside her layers of outdoor clothing.

The calf stood in a little stand of juniper trees, looking around uncertainly. As she approached, he snuffled and took a couple of steps backward.

Oh, what she'd give to be able to throw the rope she held! And to be on a horse. The calf looked bigger than it had before, and she could see that if it gave her trouble, she wasn't going to be strong enough to hold it. Darn it! It looked so easy when Marty caught one of these and easily flipped it to the ground. Maybe this hadn't been such a great idea. She just should have noted the way the calf had gone and waited for Marty.

"Here, baby," she said softly. "Are you going to come to me? I just want to take you home to Mama."

She fashioned a noose with the rope and approached a few more steps, but the calf moved away again so she stopped. Waited. Tried again. Waited again.

Now that she wasn't moving, she was starting to cool down. Fast.

She gritted her teeth. Time was passing and she was getting concerned about leaving Cheyenne alone in the house with Bobby. Though she no longer feared that her stepdaughter would harm her son, Cheyenne wasn't big enough to take care of him without help, though she *thought* she could. Juliette's biggest fear was that she would try to get him out of his crib if he woke and started to fuss.

She was starting to shiver now. She'd worn clothes for playing in the snow for a half hour or so, not the serious protection that the men wore for working out.

"All right," she said aloud. "That's it. I'm taking you home, you brat." She walked toward the calf, which backed away again. But this time Juliette didn't stop. Marching right up to the baby, she slipped the rope around its neck and turned back the way she had come.

He didn't realize she was missing until he went in for lunch. Cheyenne was at the kitchen table coloring on a big piece of butcher paper that had been taped to the tabletop. Hmm, no lunch in sight. And he was starving.

"Hey, sweet pea." Marty snatched her out of her seat and rubbed his stubbled jaw against her neck while she screamed and giggled. When he set her down again, he said, "Where's Juliette?" He figured she was probably taking care of the baby and had forgotten it was almost lunchtime.

Cheyenne was coloring again. "She went to catch a calf."

"She...what?" He wasn't sure he'd heard her right. "Tell me again."

"She went to catch the calf. You know, the one that runned the other way."

His heart almost stopped. "You mean, when we were feeding?" Good God, that had been well over an hour ago.

Cheyenne nodded. "Uh-huh." She looked up. "She told me to come in and wait for her. Maybe you better go get her, Daddy."

"Good idea." Marty was already moving toward the door. A sudden thought stopped him and he knew another moment's pure panic. "Did she take Bobby with her?"

His daughter looked scornful as if he should have known better. "No. He's napping. I listened but he hasn't waked up yet."

Relief so intense his knees felt weak rushed through him. "Okay. If he wakes up, talk to him but *do not* take him out of the crib."

He waited one second more until Cheyenne grudgingly nodded, then he was out the door. Deck had gone home to have lunch and cuddle his new daughter so he would be no help with a search.

Unless he didn't find her right away. The thought was too frightening to contemplate. He fired up the truck and tore around the corral to the gate where the calves had scattered.

And he prayed. *Please, God, don't let anything happen to Juliette....* He needed her so much. She was fragile and soft and always welcoming, and she needed him, too, in a way that Lora never had. Lora had been his helpmeet, his equal, confident, capable, strong and sure. But...

Juliette was all those things, too, in a smaller package, and he'd come to realize that a part of him was very primitive, very chauvinistic. He *liked* the way she turned to him and accepted his protection and aid. He liked the way she felt against him, small and feminine and so very, very precious. She was unique and special, and he sometimes wondered how he'd gotten so lucky.

And fear grabbed him by the throat again. *Keep her safe. Please keep her safe.*

He realized he had his eyes squeezed tightly shut and he opened them, not wanting to waste another minute of time that he could be searching.

And there in the snow was one thin line of hoof prints turning off in the opposite direction from the group he and Deck had thought were all rounded up. Damn. How had he missed that? Interspersed with the calf's prints were small, almost child-size boot prints.

And both sets only pointed in one direction. Away from the ranch buildings.

His heart skipped a beat. *Oh, God, please let her*

be all right. He alternated between cussing her lack of sense and praying for her safety as he drove up the rise of the hill as fast as he dared in four-wheel-drive. It was overcast, but at least it wasn't windy, and the tracks were plainly visible. He crested the hill and started down the other side.

And finally, there in the distance, was a tiny figure. Upright. Moving in his direction with the calf on a rope following along.

He closed his eyes for a second as he stepped on the gas, relief so intense he narrowed his eyes against the sting of tears. She was all right!

As he came closer, he stepped on the brake and stopped the truck, hurling himself out before the engine had fully died.

"What the hell did you think you were doing?" he yelled as he advanced on his wife. The calf behind her took offense to his tone and planted its feet, jerking Juliette to a stop. But Marty didn't even notice. He rushed to her side and grabbed her in a crushing embrace. "Don't you *ever* scare me like that again!"

He dropped his head and found her mouth, kissing her hard, frantically pushing his tongue into her mouth, almost sagging with relief as she stirred and turned her face more fully up to his. He changed the angle of the kiss, then pressed quick, hard kisses to her throat, her cheeks, her chin. "I'm so damned glad to see you, angel," he muttered.

The calf was pulling at the rope, almost tugging Juliette from his arms, and Marty took the rope in one hand. He kept the other firmly around her, feeling the warmth of her breath in the hollow of his neck where his jacket still hung open because he'd forgotten to zip it when he'd come out of the house again.

"I—I'm s-s-sorry." Her voice was strained. "I thought...I was afraid the c-calf would die, so I just went after it."

He realized then that she was shaking, that her face and her nose were bitter cold. And that scared him all over again. "I've got to get you warm." He dragged both calf and wife to the truck, setting Juliette inside and lifting the calf in. "Hold him." Then he jumped behind the wheel and flipped the heater on high as he turned the truck and headed back to the house.

At the corral he stopped just long enough to open the gate and shove the calf inside. A lone heifer stood by the fence, and she rushed over to take charge of her little runaway as Marty lifted Juliette out of the truck and carried her to the house.

He shouldered open the back door and set her on her feet in the utility room as he kicked the door shut with one booted foot. He ripped off his heavy gloves and dropped them and began tearing open the zipper and fastenings of her coat, unwinding the scarf from around her throat, throwing everything on the floor as he peeled away her clothing.

His fingers were shaking, and it wasn't from the cold. He took several deep breaths, trying to calm his racing pulse. She was here. She was safe.

Cheyenne came running into the room. "You're back! Did you get the calf?"

Marty nodded. "She did. And now she's going to get a hot shower."

"Is Bobby awake yet?" It was the first time Juliette had spoken since he'd brought her in.

Cheyenne nodded. "I told him you were lost."

Marty pulled Juliette into the bathroom.

"Wait!" she said. "I have to get Bobby."

Grimly he held her by one wrist as he turned the shower on and adjusted the hot water. "You have to get in that shower and warm up," he said, starting on the buttons of her shirt.

"But—"

"I'll get the kid, okay?"

She ceased struggling, and the hissing of the shower water was the only sound in the heavy silence as her big blue eyes searched his face for a long moment. Finally she nodded. "All right. I'll hurry."

He was so thankful that nothing had happened to her...so thankful. He reached for her, putting his hands at her waist and dragging her to him, then sliding his arms around her to pull her tight against his body. "God, you scared me," he muttered into her hair.

She wrapped her arms around his back and burrowed against him. "I scared me, too," she confessed. "It was a stupid thing to do. I'm sorry."

He drew back after a moment, his gaze traveling down her body where her shirt hung open. The swell of her breasts was visible beneath the scant covering of a red lacy bra, and he trailed a finger down her throat to the valley between her breasts. "Do me a favor and put this back on after your shower."

She smiled, stretching up on tiptoe to press a soft, moist kiss just below his earlobe, and he felt the whisk of her tongue across his sensitive flesh. "Anything for you."

He shuddered. "Brat. Just wait till tonight."

"With pleasure." She smiled even more widely as he released her and then spoiled the effect by shivering convulsively.

"Get in that shower and stay in there until I come back," he ordered. And with that, he shut the bathroom door in her face. He'd have liked nothing more than to climb right into that shower with her and wrap her around him right there while the water beat down on them and he warmed her from the inside out, but he had things to see to.

A baby to deal with.

He walked into the kitchen. No Cheyenne. She wasn't in the living room, either, and he began to get concerned as he heard Bobby crying. He would tan her little hide if she'd disobeyed him and was trying to handle that baby. The thought made his feet move faster and he took the steps two at a time.

Normally he'd have hesitated to enter the room where Bobby slept, but anxiety and adrenaline pushed him into the room and across to the crib before he gave himself time to think about it. Cheyenne was standing near the head of the crib, waving a stuffed animal in the air and talking to the baby, but his volume only increased.

Marty leaned over the crib and looked down at the tiny, red-faced occupant. "Hey, little man, what's the matter?"

Bobby stopped crying. His eyes widened. Whether it was the unfamiliar face in his field of vision or Marty's deep voice was debatable.

And then he smiled. Not a tentative smile, but a wriggling, fist-waving, feet-kicking, face-splitting grin. He opened his mouth and squealed happily.

"He likes you, Daddy!" Cheyenne said.

"Yeah." It was a whisper. Marty's throat grew tight. A shaft of the familiar pain speared his heart, but he forced himself to reach down and slide his big hands beneath the baby, lifting him up and settling him against his chest. The little body felt firm and warm and cuddly, and after arching his back and looking into Marty's face, the baby snuggled in as if he belonged there.

Maybe he did. Marty blinked, trying to clear vision suddenly suspiciously blurred. This child was a member of his family, *his* child now. Bobby needed him.

"He prob'ly wants his diaper changed." Cheyenne spoke with the worldly assurance of one who'd seen this ritual many times.

Marty nodded. He carried the baby over to the changing table and laid him down, looking fully for the first time at his features. Blond hair, blue eyes with the look of his mother, a dimple in one soft cheek…he was a pretty cute little critter.

He told him so, and Bobby wriggled and squealed some more. Old habits came back more easily than he'd expected, and in moments he had the little guy clean and dry. "Let's go down and find your mama," he said, scooping Bobby up and settling him in his arm. The little guy must be almost five months old now, and though he still couldn't sit up alone, he was pretty good at holding himself upright in Marty's arm, looking about with interest as they descended the stairs with Cheyenne dancing along ahead of them.

* * *

Despite her promise Juliette rushed through her shower, turning the water off as soon as she dared. She had just finished toweling herself dry and had wrapped herself in one of the man-size bath sheets when the bathroom door opened again and Marty came in.

He was carrying Bobby.

She stared, tried to speak, and stared some more. Bobby was looking around from his new vantage point, clearly pleased with himself, and when he saw her he squealed happily.

"I changed him." Marty sounded as if it were an everyday occurrence. "And Cheyenne's making open-face turkey sandwiches for lunch."

That got her attention. "What?"

"Well," he said, "She's buttering the bread. I told her I'd come and help her in a minute. Why don't you go put on something warm?"

She nodded, still staring at him holding her son. "Do you, uh, want me to take him?"

Marty shrugged. "Nah. I'll put him in his seat until you get back down here." He made no move to hand over Bobby.

She was strangely reluctant to leave her son with Marty. He didn't really like him, after all, and though she understood the pain that plagued her husband, she was uneasy about asking him to care for her son.

The thoughts must have shown on her face because Marty sent her a gentle smile, his blue eyes warm and...loving? "It's all right," he said. "Go get dressed."

So she did. But as she climbed the stairs and put

on warm, dry clothing, she couldn't forget the look in his eye. He'd never looked at her quite that way before. She would have remembered if he had.

Was it possible that Marty could grow to love her? She was almost afraid to hope. Life had knocked the pins from beneath her once before, when the husband she'd loved had died without ever even seeing their child. She'd known when she married Marty that he still loved his first wife's memory, and she'd resigned herself to it.

But that look in his eye...

Late in the afternoon she put Cheyenne down for a nap after reading her a story. Bobby was lying on his back on a blanket in the living room where they'd been playing on the floor with him. Inky lounged beside him, warily eyeing the flailing limbs. She walked upstairs with Cheyenne and tucked her in.

When she came back down the stairs, she was carrying a basket of towels to be washed. She glanced into the living to check on Bobby, who could only roll one way so far—

And stopped in her tracks.

Marty lay on the floor beside her son. He was propped on one elbow and one large hand was splayed across Bobby's midsection, lightly rubbing. Bobby had his neck stretched back and his gaze was fixed on the man who loomed over him.

Tears ran down Marty's face.

Her heart began to beat so fast she thought she might faint. Slowly she set down the basket of laundry and moved across the room to kneel at his side. At the touch of her hand, Marty turned from the baby and sat up, reaching for her. She folded her arms around his head and hugged him to her breast as his shoulders shook.

It seemed forever that they sat that way, until he was quiet against her.

"I—I'm so, so sorry," he said hoarsely.

"I'm sorry, too," she said quietly, stroking his back and running her fingers through his thick curls.

He drew back a little and looked at her. "I should have been up front with you from the very beginning."

"And I should have told you I came with baggage," she said. "But we're working it out. It's going to be okay."

"It's going to be more than okay," Marty turned and looked down at Bobby again. "How long before he can sit up?"

She shrugged. "The books say six months, which means he's got three or four weeks yet. Why?"

He smiled, his dimples flashing, and she was staggered by the uninhibited happiness in his morning-sky eyes. "Because once he can sit up, I can put him up on a horse."

"In your dreams!" But she was laughing. "I guess he can learn to ride at the same time his mother does."

Marty's face sobered at her words. "Promise me you'll never go far on foot again."

She could see the shadows that haunted his eyes, and she nodded. "I won't. It was…an impulsive decision. I was afraid that calf would get lost and freeze to death."

"It probably would have." He cradled her against him, and they were silent for a long time as they watched Bobby squirming around on the blanket. Finally Marty cleared his throat. "If you move him into the nursery, we'll have a guest room again."

She caught her breath. She hadn't even entered that room since the day she'd arrived. "Are you sure you can deal with that?"

He nodded, his smile going soft and sad around the edges. "It'll be okay." He exhaled, and he smile grew wry. "Then you can invite the dragon to visit."

"The dragon...you mean Millicent!" She was giggling. "I don't know. She can be a little overbearing."

"So can I." Marty caressed her cheek. "You want Bobby to know his grandmother, don't you?"

As she nodded, he said, "Then let her come to visit. Trust me to take care of you, angel. I won't let her railroad you into anything."

She nodded, rubbing her cheek again his big, rough fingers. "All right."

Marty nodded in satisfaction. Then he leaned over Bobby again. "Hey, big guy, wanna play peek-a-boo?"

She laughed at the incongruity of the big broad-shouldered man playing baby games with an infant, but inside, her heart was singing. If Marty could get past his sorrow enough to love her son, surely he'd be thrilled with a child made by the two of them.

She was fairly certain she was pregnant now. Her period was a month overdue and her breasts were incredibly tender, just as they'd felt in the early stages of her first pregnancy. It would be a while, though, before she started to show. So she'd wait just a little longer before telling Marty and changing the status quo once again.

The rest of the month of March was quiet due to two more blizzards and high winds that kept drifting the roads shut, which suited Marty just fine, except for the danger to newborn calves. He and Deck moved all the heavy cows into pastures near the barn and kept a close eye on them as calving season began in earnest in April.

He pulled backward calves that were coming feet first and ones that got stuck halfway born. He tugged on heifers' tails to get exhausted, temporarily paralyzed cows back on their feet after rough births. Juliette was horrified the first time she saw him do it, until he explained that it gave the cow enough balance to get her back legs under her and get to her feet. A couple of heifers had been covered by the neighbor's wandering Charolais bull, and he and Deck both cussed and swore as the cows struggled to deliver the too-large calves. Twice he had to call the vet, once to deliver a dead calf by C-section and once to replace a prolapsed uterus. He was gratified that both the cow and calf survived that one.

He taught Juliette how to walk through the herd looking for cows with larger-than-normal bags, which might mean a sick calf that wasn't sucking. She quickly developed an amazing talent for seeing which calves were getting sick—something that he'd never figured out until they were lying too still—and they were able to shove scours pills into them so fast that they only lost a few.

Most of the time he was too tired to think, which

was just as well. He rose in the dark, fed, medicated and birthed cattle all day, and he fell into bed at night only to rise and go through the same routine again and again. He and Juliette made love in the mornings, when his desire for her would beat back the exhaustion for a while, and her calm management of the house made calving season easier than it had been since Lora died. Still, he felt like someone had knocked him down and stomped all over him. Figuratively, if not literally.

He hadn't felt this...battered emotionally since Lora and the baby had died.

He was filled with a puzzling blend of gladness and old sorrow, though the sorrow receded a little more with each day that passed, each new memory that eased the pain of the old ones. He felt guilty sometimes, afraid that he was forgetting. Then rationality took over and he knew life had to go on. Lora would have wanted him to be happy again.

And despite the tiring work, his days *were* happy now, filled with those special moments that only parents know when a baby does something new and wondrous for the first time. Bobby sat up alone on the fifteenth of April, and when Juliette's gaze met his across the living room as they laughed at the triumphant expression on the little guy's face, he felt something in his heart click into place, something that had been missing for more than two years.

Or maybe, if he was honest, he'd never known quite this feeling before.

He loved her. God, how he loved her! She'd come with him, stayed with him despite almost impossible circumstances, when any other woman would have given up and left. She'd made his house a home again and taken his daughter into her heart as her own. He'd never expected or demanded that she get involved with as much of the actual work of ranching, but she was doing that, too.

She was still fragile and alluring and wide-eyed and so sweet that he caught himself wanting her more than could possibly be good for either of them. It was probably a good thing he had work and they had kids to deal with, because if they'd been typical carefree newlyweds, he had a feeling they'd have worn out a couple of mattresses by now.

He couldn't remember ever having quite the same desperate need for Lora. Sure, he'd wanted her. They'd been young when they started dating and not much older when they'd gotten married. But...the bottom line was that he'd survived when Lora had died, had been able to somehow go on. Had been able to find this woman whom he now could admit that he loved. And whom he knew, deep down in his heart, loved him with the same intensity. Though he'd never encouraged her to say the words, her actions, the look in her beautiful blue eyes, the staggering passion she offered him along with her slim, perfect body all told him she loved him.

And he knew if anything ever happened to Juliette, nothing else in the world would ever matter again. He would tell her so, he promised himself, just as soon as calving season was over and he could take half a day off. Deck owed him, from the summer before when he'd been courting Silver, and he thought it might be nice to simply take a picnic down by the river, tell her how he felt…and then make love to her until neither one of them could walk.

The idea filled him with immense satisfaction, and he whistled as he went about his work in the last few days of April.

By the first of May there were only a few dozen cows still to calve, and Marty told her he thought the worst was past. There was still branding, of course, but the days were getting longer and the temperatures were sneaking higher with each week that passed. The low had actually been above freezing a time or two, and everyone was feeling giddy at making it through winter.

Juliette called Millicent as Marty had suggested. The older woman had leaped at the invitation to visit. She'd been significantly less abrasive and she'd actually asked a number of questions about how old Cheyenne was and what kinds of things she liked to do. If Juliette knew her former mother-in-law, Millicent would arrive on her doorstep with enough gifts to bribe any child. But even that prospect wasn't daunting. Millicent had been far less demanding since Marty had recommended that she quit making threats. Regardless of how it happened, Juliette was thankful for the change.

She'd begun gardening, as well. It was the first time she'd grown anything other than flowers and Lyn had been advising her. The two women had transplanted asparagus weeks ago, put in lettuce and radishes that were just starting to appear as the snow melted, and on one particularly warm day, she planted onions and potatoes in the soggy ground.

Cheyenne was over at Silver's for the day, "helping" with her cousin Erica, and Bobby was down for his afternoon nap, which usually lasted a solid two hours. She got the vegetables in and came back to the house covered with sticky mud.

Marty saw her crossing the yard to the back door. He smiled and waved from where he was working on the tractor, and she blew him a kiss, then made a face when she tasted mud on her lips from her fingertips. She could still hear his laughter as she went inside.

She stripped off everything in the utility room. It was strange how quickly she'd gotten accustomed to the isolation of the ranch. She would never have considered walking around naked before, for fear someone would come to the door or peep through a window. The muddiest clothing she dumped in the sink and rinsed, then she threw everything in the washing machine. After Marty came in and changed, she would do a load of the things they'd worn today. It was, she'd discovered, the only real method of keeping up with the interminable loads of filthy clothing a ranch seemed to generate.

As she entered the bathroom and got ready to shower, she congratulated herself on having the foresight to bring her robe downstairs that morning and hang it on the back of the bathroom door. She was plenty warm now from her exertions, but she knew from experience that she'd cool down fast, and the air was still chilly enough to be uncomfortable.

The shower felt heavenly as she rinsed away the grit and mud, shampooed her hair and lingered over soaping herself. When the shower curtain opened suddenly, she screamed and nearly dropped the soap.

Marty roared with laughter as he stepped into the shower stall, crowding her back against the wall. He was stark naked and beautiful, heavily aroused—he'd clearly been thinking of joining her. He grabbed the soap and slicked his hands with it, then began to rub her shoulders. "Hi, there," he said.

She placed her hands against the hard pads of muscle defining his chest, exhaling in relief. "Hi. You scared me silly."

"Sorry." His blue eyes were gleaming.

She'd never seen a man look *less* sorry about anything in his life. Slipping her arms up around his neck, she brought her body closer to his. "Mmm, I've missed you."

"I've missed you, too." His breathing was growing labored. He turned her around so that her back was to him and pressed her back against his body and she could feel him solid and throbbing against her. "But calving's done now and we have time..."

He rubbed his soapy palms over her breasts, and she couldn't prevent the small sound that escaped as he circled the sensitive peaks and sent sensation soaring through her. She was so much smaller than he that he could easily look over her shoulder and she tilted her head back against his strong chest and let him look his fill. It had been so long since they'd had time for anything more than hasty but satisfying couplings stolen in the early-morning moments before he had to get to work.

His hands moved down her body, shaping the flare of her hips and then sliding around to meet between her thighs, and he gently widened her stance so that he could touch her there. She moaned then, and as his questing, circling fingers pleasured her, she let herself go, moving her hips in time with his petting. The growing swell of sensual excitement pushed her higher and higher, and when he suddenly plunged one finger deep inside her, she reacted immediately, shuddering with her own completion as her body heaved in his arms.

Marty's breathing came in hoarse gasps as he turned her to face him. He reached behind her head and retrieved a small foil package from the shelf where he'd place it, and his hands shook as he tore it open. She took it from him, gently stroking the protection into place until he was groaning, gripping her waist and lifting her. He pinned her between his big hard body and the cool wall of the shower stall, and she gasped at the temperature of the cold tiles. Then she gasped again and forgot all about the chill as he reached between them and pushed himself inside her, his sturdy length a hot contrast to the cool wall, filling her so full that she could only wrap her legs around him and helplessly hold on to his shoulders as he began to thrust steadily in and out, moving her up and down on him with his hands on her hips and his head thrown back. The world receded to that one point of contact, of sensation, and she felt herself gathering taut again, exploding again before he increased his rhythm and brought himself to a plunging, driving finish, his heavy strength pushing her hard against the wall as he emptied himself deep inside her.

He held her there for a long time until his breathing settled again. Finally he lifted her off him, wincing as the warm shower water sluiced over his sensitive flesh. He reached out and turned off the water, then whipped two towels over the top of the shower door, wrapping her in one as if she were a child. He took a moment to discard the protection he'd used before anchoring the other towel at his waist, and she had a moment's guilty disquiet. She had to tell him soon about her pregnancy. She'd put it off far too long already. Maybe tonight...

Then he lifted her into his arms, unlocking the bathroom door and carrying her up the stairs to their bedroom. "How much longer have we got?" he asked, indicating Bobby's closed bedroom door as they passed it.

She kissed his throat. "Maybe an hour?"

"Not nearly enough," he said, "but I guess we'll have to make the most of it." His blue eyes were warm and brilliant as he looked down at her, and her breath caught in her throat. She'd seen that look more and more often recently. And though she tried to tell herself not to read things into a simple glance, she couldn't help but think that some part of Marty's heart was opening to her at last.

He set her on her feet beside the bed, in a shaft of bright afternoon sunlight that streamed through the window, drawing the towel away. "I want to look at you," he said. "It's been too long."

Alarm bells suddenly clanged in her mind. She was almost four months along now and finally starting to show a little, though she was sure he hadn't realized it. She clutched at the towel, but he was too strong, and he pulled it away from her laughing.

Then his laughter stopped—abruptly, as if someone

had put a hand over his mouth. As his eyes narrowed, then widened in stunned incredulity, she saw that he recognized her pregnant state now.

And he didn't look happy about it.

Eight

"**Y**ou're pregnant." His voice was flat and wooden, his eyes devoid of any warmth. He eyed her belly with the same look she'd expect him to use on a rattlesnake.

His reaction was so far from the few fleeting imaginings of she'd allowed herself that she simply stood, stunned, too hurt to draw breath, until she realized she was cold. She felt naked, horribly, pathetically vulnerable. Turning away from him, she grabbed for her robe hanging at the foot of the bed and fumbled herself into it. "Yes."

Marty ran a shaking hand through his hair. "Dammit, Juliette! We never talked about having more children." His voice grew louder, angrier. "How in hell could you do something like this to me?"

She whirled around, stung by the accusation. "It

was an accident,'' she said fiercely. ''I didn't do 'this' to you!''

''I don't want more children,'' he said harshly, slashing her heart to ribbons with the angry words, and she let her own anger rise, let her control snap, anything to deflect the searing pain his callous attitude inflicted.

''Well then, you should have stayed out of the pantry!'' she yelled at him.

''The pantry…'' She could see it the moment he remembered. He swore, a low, vicious stream. Then he speared her with a look. ''How far along are you?''

''Almost sixteen weeks.'' She concentrated every ounce of her energy on holding her shattered emotions in check.

''Oh, sweet heaven.'' Marty sank down on the side of the bed, covering his face with his hands. ''I don't want more children.''

The ugly words fell into the growing chasm between them.

Every hope, every dream she'd had of the future, every idealistic notion of a loving lifetime with this man died in that moment. Backing away from him, she groped for the frame of the bathroom door.

She saw him realize what she was doing, but she was already in the bathroom by then, and she slammed and locked the door seconds before he could spring across the room. On the other side he was shouting, roaring something, but she closed her ears to his demands and turned on both the sink and the shower, running precious drops of water to drown out his voice.

He stayed there until she turned off the water. She

steadfastly ignored his demands for her to open the door, but finally he swore and slammed both fists against the frame so hard it shook and she jumped. Then she heard his booted feet moving out of the room and down the hallway. She listened intently, peeking through the curtains of the single window as she heard the back door slam, and then she could see him striding across the yard to the barn.

Her chest ached with unreleased sobs, but she couldn't afford to cry right now or she might never stop. Deliberately she blanked him from her mind, concentrating instead on the task at hand. With quick economic motions, she dressed and dragged one of her suitcases out of the closet where they'd been stored. She packed practical clothing, enough for a few days, then went into Bobby's room and quietly got his things together. As she came back into the bedroom to put them in the suitcase, the sound of a jingling bridle drew her to the window. Marty was on his favorite gelding and as she watched, he rode off toward the ridge. The last sight she had of her husband was of his straight back in the saddle as he disappeared behind the hill.

She used the telephone by the bed, making one call to Rapid City Regional Airport and one more to Lyn. Then she packed and dragged her suitcase downstairs. Swiftly she moved around the kitchen, picking out the things she'd need for Bobby.

On the refrigerator hung a piece of butcher paper with a finger-painting that Cheyenne had done. The tears almost got away from her as she took it down and carefully laid it flat atop the things in the suitcase, but she took deep breaths until she felt the steely calm descend again.

She was pregnant. *Oh, God. Oh, God.* What was he going to do if he lost her?

Marty's breath came in short, gasping pants as if he'd been running instead of riding. In his mind's eye, a truck bounced across the rough ground and skidded to a stop beside him. Lora's face was drawn with pain and fear.

"I'm in labor."

He'd been stunned. "But…you're not due until—"

"You tell the baby that. *I'm* going to the hospital *now!*" She'd been screaming at him by the end of the sentence, and he'd quickly moved into action, turning his horse loose and sliding behind the wheel.

He'd called Deck on the car phone to come collect the horse and turned the truck toward Rapid City, praying the whole way.

But his prayers had gone unanswered. God, he'd never felt so helpless in his entire life. So sick, so devastated. A thousand times since then he'd asked himself what he could have done, *should* have done differently. He'd tortured himself with fantasies in which he stanched the flow of blood and saved his wife.

But he hadn't. She'd died, and so had their baby boy.

It was only since meeting Juliette that he'd begun to believe that maybe his story could have a happy ending, that maybe he could reclaim his life through the greatest love he'd ever known—and now she was pregnant.

God, what if she died?

He'd survived Lora's death but if anything happened to Juliette…

And it could. It could. His vivid imagination conjured up dozens of equally hellish scenarios. They lived too far from the hospital. She was tiny, so damned tiny. She should never be trying to bear a child. Lora had hemorrhaged. So could Juliette.

He could still see the horrified look on her face when he'd blurted out his first panicky, stupid reaction.

Irrational anger rose to choke him. How could she have done it? he'd asked her. Oh, he knew, all right. Knew what she'd said about the pantry. And he remembered the hot, slick, incredibly perfect moments when he'd sunk deep into her with nothing between them. Hell, he'd thought about that particular day more times over the past few months than could possibly be normal. If she just wasn't so damned enticing…! All he'd been able to think of since she'd come to live with him was sex. Making love to her. Morning, noon and night, he'd had Juliette on his mind.

And now look what he had to show for it. A marriage in ruins and a wife…he nearly whimpered aloud. A wife who easily could lose her life because of his carelessness.

He slowed the gelding to a leisurely walk as his conscience bit at him and the anger fell away. This was no more her fault than it was his. She'd looked so shattered…she was probably sitting there crying her eyes out right now. As frightened as he was, he couldn't let her go through this alone.

Determination firmed his mouth. He was taking her to a doctor *today*. And he wasn't letting her out of his sight until this baby was born.

This baby. A small thrill ran through him, grew and spread. If he weren't so damned afraid for her, he'd be loopy with happiness. A child made from the two of them, from their love. His aching heart softened. Another little girl? Or a brother for Bobby?

Oh, God, please don't let anything happen to my wife. I need her. I love her. I need her to love me.

"Yo! Marty!" A faint voice from over the ridge made him slow the gelding and listen. The voice came again, deep, masculine and anxious. Cal.

He reined in his mount and stopped as Cal came over the ridge on the big bay he often rode, riding fast and steady until he got to where Marty was waiting.

His friend's gray eyes were watchful as he neared. "What are you doing out here?"

He didn't think he could share his private agony with anyone right now. "I'm a cowboy. I work out here, remember?"

"Yeah? Well, while you're working out here your wife's catching a plane to California."

Fresh shock rippled through him. *"What?"*

"Lyn called me and suggested I get out here and find you. Juliette asked to her to drive her to the airport. Lyn said she'd do it, but she's stalling." Cal eyed him, frowning. "You want to tell me what in hell is going on? Last time I looked, you and your pretty little wife were about as cozy as a couple can get.''

No, he *didn't* want to tell Cal anything. But the two had grown up together, and if there was one thing he knew about Cal McCall, it was that the man could sit there and never say another word until a fellow felt so guilty he couldn't stand it.

''We had a fight,'' he muttered. Panic was rising as Cal's words sank in. She was *leaving?* She couldn't leave! He loved her.

Cal raised one dark eyebrow. ''Must've been some fight for her to be leaving. You said something stupid, didn't you?''

Marty eyed him sourly. ''Oh, like you've never done anything dumb in the name of romance.''

Cal grinned. ''I'm a man. According to Lyn, that says it all.'' Then his face sobered. ''Come on. If you want to stop her, we'd better get moving. No, not back to the house,'' he said as Marty turned his horse. ''Better try to catch them at the end of the lane.''

Cal's truck pulled into the yard with Lyn behind the wheel. She slid out of the cab and hurried across the yard to the house.

Juliette met her at the front door. ''Thank you,'' she said quietly.

''Don't thank me yet,'' Lyn said. ''What's the matter between you and Marty? Have you tried to talk it out? I know life out here can be tough, but you've made it through the first winter and calving season and I thought—''

''I'm pregnant.'' The dull, flat words cut Lyn off in midsentence, and her green eyes widened.

"Well, then surely—"

"Marty doesn't want it."

Lyn recoiled. "Are you sure? I thought Bobby was growing on him." She held up her hands helplessly. "I know he might think it's a little soon since you just got married and you already have two—"

"No. He just—doesn't want any more children. At all."

Lyn's mouth fell open. "You're kidding."

"He said so." Juliette shook her head, swallowing the lump that was growing too large to speak around. "I have to catch a plane. If you drive me, Marty won't have to come pick up the truck."

Lyn hesitated. Nodded. "All right."

Juliette set Inky's small crate into the back of the truck and began throwing her things in after it. Then she went upstairs and got Bobby. He needed to be changed and dressed, and she began to fret about the time, fearing that Marty might return. It wasn't so much that she worried he would stop her from leaving, but she didn't want any more big scenes.

Her chin trembled and she bit down fiercely on her lower lip until the pain distracted her enough to get the tears under control. She could cry later. Right now she had to get off this ranch.

When she went back downstairs, Lyn was waiting in the living room. She stood as Juliette came into the room. "Maybe I'd better use your bathroom before we leave. It's a long drive to Rapid, and my bladder's feeling a bit squished these days." The tall redhead rested a hand on the gentle swell of her abdomen, still barely noticeable though she was almost six months pregnant. "I guess you know what that's like."

Juliette nodded, not trusting her voice. She'd come to care for both Lyn and Silver, and she would miss them. She took Bobby out and put him in his car seat, strapping it securely into Lyn's truck.

A few minutes later Lyn came out onto the porch. "One more minute," she called, holding up a finger. "Cal's out, but I need to leave him a message so he knows I'll be gone for a while." And she disappeared into the house again.

It seemed to take forever, but she finally returned, carefully shutting the door behind her. She picked her way through the snowy patches to the truck with a great deal more care than she'd shown rushing in. Then she had to find the keys, which she finally located wedged in a bottom pocket of her bib overalls beneath her coat.

By this time Juliette's senses were screaming at her to *go,* but she gritted her teeth and didn't comment on the need to hurry. Marty could return any minute.

At last Lyn got the truck in gear, and they started out the lane. Juliette felt some of the tension leaving her taut muscles with every yard of distance covered, though she knew she wouldn't really relax until she was on that plane to California.

Her heart sank even more, if that were possible, at the thought of facing Millicent, pregnant and practically destitute. The only good thing that would come of it would be that Bobby would get to know his paternal grandmother, and if Juliette were vigilant and firm, Millicent wouldn't take over his life the way she had his father's. The very idea was daunting, and she closed her eyes and laid her head wearily against the seat back as Lyn bumped the truck out the lane.

When the truck slowed a few minutes later, she opened her eyes expecting to see the highway. But they weren't at the end of the ranch road yet.

Two horsemen sat astride their mounts, blocking the lane.

Lyn scrambled out of the cab before Juliette could even absorb the betrayal and ran to her husband, who'd dismounted.

Juliette sat perfectly still for a long moment. She refused to look at the other man who still sat his horse. Then she, too, got out of the truck. She walked toward the three people, the full weight of humiliation and despair making each step an effort. Marty had made it clear he didn't want her child. He'd never said he loved her, either, and while she'd thought that wouldn't matter when they'd married, she knew now it wouldn't be enough for the rest of her life.

"Juliette." Marty's voice cut through the awkward silence. "We have to talk."

She ignored him, advancing on Cal. "How did you—Lyn told you!" She turned to the other woman, and her eyes glistened with tears. "I thought you were my friend," she said bitterly. "I guess I should have known better. It was stupid of me to think I could depend on Marty's friends for anything."

Cal put a comforting arm around his wife's shoulder. "We're your friends, too," he said quietly. "That's why we hated to see you leave without at least trying to talk things out with Marty."

She wouldn't look at him. Her lovely face was chilly and as severe as a marble statue.

He'd known it would be hard, but suddenly a fear even greater than the others he'd lived with shot through him, chilling him to the bone. *What if she wouldn't listen?* What if she listened and left anyway?

Marty's horse shifted restlessly, probably picking up on his own roiling, unsettled emotions. The cold fist of fear around his heart didn't ease, but the irrational anger that had gripped him since he'd seen Juliette standing in that shaft of sunlight, the backlit window illuminating her slender body and the slight but frighteningly distinct swell of her abdomen, had dissipated. He glanced down at Cal, standing with his wife's face turned into his shoulder.

His friend.

"Would you take the truck back to the house?" he asked. "And keep an eye on the baby for a while?"

Cal nodded.

Juliette crossed her arms. "I need that truck. I have a plane to catch."

Lyn didn't look at any of them as she climbed back into the cab of the truck and turned around, then headed back toward the ranch with Bobby in the infant seat beside her. Cal mounted his horse and followed, and in a moment they'd moved over a small hill and out of sight.

Juliette stood watching until they were gone. Then she squared her shoulders and turned her back on Marty. Resolutely she began to walk back along the lane.

"Juliette, wait. We need to talk." He repeated his earlier words.

"You said everything there was to say already." Her words floated back to him. She didn't stop.

Damn! He'd never seen her so icy cold, so angry. Still, he wasn't quitting. He urged his horse forward, going around her a small distance and dismounting in front of her.

"You're not going anywhere until you listen to me," he informed her.

She stopped in her tracks, clearly unwilling to get too close to him. "Fine. I'll walk to the road and get help from someone." Belligerently, she turned her back on him and started walking away again.

All right. That was it. He'd *had* it. He started after her. Too late, she realized he was coming and she started to run but he caught her within a dozen steps, whirling her against him and into his arms.

"Let me go!" It was a shriek, and he was shocked by the genuine fury she showed as she fought to free herself. He dedicated himself to subduing her without hurting her much as he would a new calf. Finally, tired of her squirming, he pinned her arms to her sides and yanked her hard against him so that she couldn't kick him.

She froze. So did he. Her body was soft, cushioning him where he pressed her close. The air was electric, filled with the sound of their ragged breathing. Her gaze dropped to his mouth, and an erotic jolt shot straight to his groin. His body was already hard and excited by the struggle with her warm female form, and he suddenly moved again, firmly covering her lips with his and molding them, thrusting his tongue between her teeth again and again until the rigid resistance left her body and she was kissing him back.

He bent and lifted her into his arms, then walked her three steps out of the lane and onto a sweet grassy bed thick with tiny bluebells, careful to set her down gently.

"Will you let me go?" Her words were filled with pain.

"Not until you listen to me." Breathing hard, he looked down into her face.

And was shocked again.

She was crying. Huge tears rolled back into her hair. Her blue eyes met his and in their depths he read a deep, indescribable sorrow that rocked him to his core.

He groaned. "Don't cry, angel. It tears my heart out when you cry."

"You don't ha-have a heart." The words were sobs. "No one w-with a heart would say he didn't want his own child."

"I know." He pulled back from her, then gathered her close, rocking her gently, absorbing her pain. "I didn't mean it. I don't even know why I said that."

"You wouldn't have said it if you didn't mean it." Her voice was muffled in his throat. She wasn't fighting him anymore, but she wasn't embracing him back, and that shaft of naked fear shot through him again. She sounded so...so hopeless.

Had he ruined the best thing ever to enter his life by allowing his own stupid fears to rule him?

"I didn't mean it," he said again. Quietly. He sighed, pulling her back and putting his thumb beneath her chin to lift her face to his. When her eyes met his, he let everything he was feeling show. "I was terrified," he said slowly, forcing the words past the lump in his throat. "Terrified of losing you. Thinking about you having a baby…you're so fragile and delicate. And we're so far away from the hospital here." He swallowed. "I can't live without you. I *can't*. I love you. I love you so much that if something happened to you it would kill me." His voice was little more than a harsh whisper. "After Lora died, I hurt but I kept on going. I had Cheyenne to think about, and somewhere in the back of my mind I always knew I'd get married again some day. I planned it all out but I couldn't find the right woman. When I met you, everything fell into place."

"Marty—"

He shook his head and laid a gentle finger against her lips, looking deep into her eyes. "I *do* want this baby. A part of me wants nothing more than a living, breathing symbol of how much I love you. But I wouldn't be honest if I didn't tell you that another part of me is scared absolutely spitless by the thought of you trying to deliver our child." His voice broke, and he had to stop and swallow again. "I can't lose you."

Tears were still rolling from her eyes, but she raised her hands and cupped his jaw, and he briefly closed his eyes in relief as he read her expression.

"I love you," she said. "I loved you from the first day we met, even though I told myself I was crazy, that love at first sight was just an expression. I could never be sorry that your baby is growing inside me."

Shaken to the core, humbled by her unflagging love for him, he turned his head and kissed her palm.

"We can take all the precautions you want," she said, "I'll move to town and live beside the hospital if it will make you feel better, but you have to relax and not worry so much. I've already had one child, remember? My labor was only six hours long and I barely remember pushing. It was an extremely easy birth, and he weighed over eight pounds. The doctor told me I was made for having babies. I can do this,'' she told him softly. "*We* can do this."

Did he dare allow himself to be convinced, comforted, by her words? He dropped his head and sought her mouth for a slow, sweet kiss. "I want to believe it."

"Then let yourself," she said. "We're going to have a whole lifetime together. With our children."

He whistled for his horse, and when it was standing at his side, he lifted his wife and set her in the saddle, then swung up behind her. "Let's go home."

"Home," she echoed, and he put his hand under her jaw and turned her face to his so that he could kiss her.

"Thank you," he said, "for loving me."

"It wasn't hard." Her eyes were shining.

Deliberately he moved against her bottom, snuggled against him in the deep saddle. "It is now."

And they laughed again before he kissed her as the horse carried them home.

Epilogue

It was a christening party.

"There. The guest of honor is clean, dry and fed again," Juliette said as she carried three-month-old Analisa back out to the group gathered beneath the big shade trees in the yard.

"That's the way we like 'em," Deck said. He rose to his feet. "I'd better go help Cal and Marty with that riding lesson. Looks like they've got their hands full." He gestured down toward the corral where the two men were juggling a group of children and two horses.

"Here." Silver rose and settled their year-old daughter Genie in his arm. "Hang on to this one and see how Erica's doing while I help clear the tables."

Lyn looked up from her chair, where she was nursing her third child, six-month-old Jonathan. "Wait till he's done eating and I'll help you."

"Sounds like a deal." Silver settled back in her chair and chuckled. "Hey. How'd I do that? No kids!"

All three women laughed softly. "I'm not sure I remember what that's like," Juliette said ruefully. She looked down toward the pasture where Cheyenne, who was even more strikingly lovely at eight than she'd been at four, was carrying Lyn's middle child, Julia, around in the pasture. Cal and Lyn's kids were easy to spot; they all had their mother's deep-red curls.

"Actually, you and Marty never had a chance to spend time together without kids," Silver pointed out. "You won't know what to do with yourselves when all five of them are grown and gone.

Juliette arched an eyebrow and smiled. "Oh, I imagine we'll find something to do."

Lyn snorted hard enough to startle baby Jonathan, whose tiny hand flew out reflexively before he settled back down to nurse. "You two are positively indecent! Didn't anyone ever tell you grown-ups aren't supposed to neck in the back of the car and smooch in public all the time?"

Silver was laughing, too. "Hmm, if that isn't the pot calling the kettle black. Aren't you the one with three children under the age of three?" She rose. "I think I'll start these dishes before I get *myself* in trouble here."

"I'll help, too. Just let me take Analisa down to Marty." Juliette rose and started down toward the corral. Inside, Marty and Cal each held a docile mare.

Cal's horse carried his three-year-old niece Erica and his own son, Jason, just half a year younger.

Marty was close to his mount, keeping an eagle eye on what she could only think was a portrait labeled *Trouble on Horseback*. Bobby, a four-and-a-half-year-old whirlwind, sat in front. Behind him rode his twin brothers Aaron and Neil. She wouldn't put it past a single one of the little rascals to leap off with no warning, either, she thought fondly, looking at her sons. They were all as blond as she, though the twins had inherited their father's size and were almost as big as Bobby. People frequently exclaimed over their "triplets."

She stepped into the corral and closed the gate behind her, making her way to Marty's side as he handed the reins of the horse to Deck. "Hi, there, cowboy," she said. "Wanna make a date for tonight?"

Her husband slipped his strong arms around her, and she relaxed into the familiar embrace, shifting the baby to the side. "Sounds good to me," he said, and his eyes slipped down over her body, lingering for a moment on the neckline of the sweater she wore. "How about a little something to keep me going till later?"

She tilted her face up to his, slipping her free hand up to his neck and teasing the curls that brushed there. "Okay. Wouldn't want you to run out of energy."

As his lips descended on hers, she closed her eyes and gave herself to the familiar thrill of his touch. Unbidden, a memory of the day she'd mailed her first letter to him slipped into her head.

As he released her lips reluctantly, she said, "You

know, when I answered your ad that first time, I nearly crawled into the mailbox and fished it back out. I thought it was a huge mistake.''

"That would have been a really, really bad move.'' He shook his head. "I can't imagine my life without you, angel.''

She smiled, stretching on tiptoe to nuzzle his neck before he tilted his head and sought her lips again. "I love you.''

From the horse's back, a childish voice said, "Yuck. Daddy's kissin' Mama *again*,'' and the air was filled with the sounds of three little boys make exaggerated gagging noises.

Marty lifted his head and eyed his sons narrowly while Juliette tried her best not to laugh. "I look forward to the day when you get sloppy in love with some woman.''

"Not me,'' said Bobby stoutly. "I'm never getting married!''

"Me, neither,'' said Aaron.

"Me, neither,'' said Neil.

But their parents didn't answer. They were kissing again.

*　*　*　*　*

Desire ®

MAN OF THE MONTH

For twenty years Silhouette has been giving
you the ultimate in romantic reads. Come join
the celebration as some of your favorite authors
help celebrate our anniversary with the most
sensual, emotional love stories ever!

Available at your favorite retail outlet.

Silhouette ®

Where love comes alive ™

Visit Silhouette at www.eHarlequin.com   SDMOM01

CELEBRATE VALENTINE'S DAY WITH HARLEQUIN®'S LATEST TITLE— *Stolen Memories*

Available in trade-size format, this collector's edition contains three full-length novels by *New York Times* bestselling authors Jayne Ann Krentz and Tess Gerritsen, along with national bestselling author Stella Cameron.

TEST OF TIME by **Jayne Ann Krentz**—
He married for the best reason.... She married for the only reason.... Did they stand a chance at making the only reason the real reason to share a lifetime?

THIEF OF HEARTS by **Tess Gerritsen**—
Their distrust of each other was only as strong as their desire. And Jordan began to fear that Diana was more than just a thief of hearts.

MOONTIDE by **Stella Cameron**—
For Andrew, Greer's return is a miracle. It had broken his heart to let her go. Now fate has brought them back together. And he won't lose her again...

Make this Valentine's Day one to remember!

Look for this exciting collector's edition on sale January 2001 at your favorite retail outlet.

HARLEQUIN®
Makes any time special ™

Visit us at www.eHarlequin.com

PHSM

#1 *New York Times* bestselling author

NORA ROBERTS

brings you more of the loyal and loving,
tempestuous and tantalizing Stanislaski family.

Coming in February 2001

The Stanislaski Sisters

Natasha and Rachel

Though raised in the Old World traditions of their
family, fiery Natasha Stanislaski and cool, classy
Rachel Stanislaski are ready for a *new* world of love....

*And also available in February 2001 from
Silhouette Special Edition, the newest book in the
heartwarming Stanislaski saga*

CONSIDERING KATE

Natasha and Spencer Kimball's daughter Kate turns her
back on old dreams and returns to her hometown, where
she finds the *man* of her dreams.

Available at your favorite retail outlet.

Where love comes alive™

Silhouette —

where love comes alive—online...

eHARLEQUIN.com

your romantic
books

♥ **Shop online!** Visit Shop eHarlequin and discover a wide selection of new releases and classic favorites at great discounted prices.

♥ **Read** our daily and weekly Internet exclusive serials, and participate in our interactive novel in the reading room.

♥ **Ever dreamed** of being a writer? Enter your chapter for a chance to become a featured author in our Writing Round Robin novel.

• • • • • • •

your romantic
life

♥ **Check out** our feature articles on dating, flirting and other important romance topics and get your daily love dose with tips on how to keep the romance alive every day.

• • • • • • •

your
community

♥ **Have a Heart-to-Heart** with other members about the latest books and meet your favorite authors.

♥ **Discuss** your romantic dilemma in the Tales from the Heart message board.

your romantic
escapes

♥ **Learn** what the stars have in store for you with our daily Passionscopes and weekly Erotiscopes.

♥ **Get the latest scoop** on your favorite royals in Royal Romance.

If you enjoyed what you just read,
then we've got an offer you can't resist!

Take 2 bestselling love stories FREE!

Plus get a FREE surprise gift!

////////////////////////////////////

Clip this page and mail it to Silhouette Reader Service™

IN U.S.A.	IN CANADA
3010 Walden Ave.	P.O. Box 609
P.O. Box 1867	Fort Erie, Ontario
Buffalo, N.Y. 14240-1867	L2A 5X3

YES! Please send me 2 free Silhouette Desire® novels and my free surprise gift. Then send me 6 brand-new novels every month, which I will receive months before they're available in stores. In the U.S.A., bill me at the bargain price of $3.34 plus 25¢ delivery per book and applicable sales tax, if any*. In Canada, bill me at the bargain price of $3.74 plus 25¢ delivery per book and applicable taxes**. That's the complete price and a savings of at least 10% off the cover prices—what a great deal! I understand that accepting the 2 free books and gift places me under no obligation ever to buy any books. I can always return a shipment and cancel at any time. Even if I never buy another book from Silhouette, the 2 free books and gift are mine to keep forever. So why not take us up on our invitation. You'll be glad you did!

225 SEN C222
326 SEN C223

Name	(PLEASE PRINT)	
Address	Apt.#	
City	State/Prov.	Zip/Postal Code

* Terms and prices subject to change without notice. Sales tax applicable in N.Y.
** Canadian residents will be charged applicable provincial taxes and GST.
   All orders subject to approval. Offer limited to one per household.
   ® are registered trademarks of Harlequin Enterprises Limited.

DES00   ©1998 Harlequin Enterprises Limited

In March 2001,

Silhouette Desire

presents the next book in

DIANA PALMER's

enthralling *Soldiers of Fortune* trilogy:

THE WINTER SOLDIER

Cy Parks had a reputation around Jacobsville for his taciturn and solitary ways. But spirited Lisa Monroe wasn't put off by the mesmerizing mercenary, and drove him to distraction with her sweetly tantalizing kisses. Though he'd never admit it, Cy was getting mighty possessive of the enchanting woman who needed the type of safeguarding only he could provide. But who would protect the beguiling beauty from *him…?*

Soldiers of Fortune…prisoners of love.

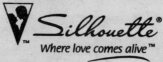